No Rest for the Weary

Somebody had told the merchant that Slocum had killed Michael Holman, giving a precise description. Something burning in his gut told him it was the same person who had shot down Macauley after sending him on an enraged mission to kill the man who was ready to run off with his wife.

"Your face changed," Angelina said in a small voice. "What does that mean? What are you going to do?"

"Help you," he said. "Whoever killed your husband likely has it in for me and is spreading rumors that I'm responsible."

"So, find who is saying all those terrible things and *that's* who killed Michael?"

Slocum couldn't say. Who died after a boulder was pushed down a hill toward a town couldn't be determined. The boulder did the killing, but it would never have started rolling if someone hadn't tipped it on its way. Slocum suspected he had to find the man with the lever rather than those with the smoking pistols.

JAKE LOGAN

SLOCUM
AND THE
MEDDLER

JOVE BOOKS, NEW YORK

WESTERN LOG

THE BERKLEY PUBLISHING GROUP
Published by the Penguin Group
Penguin Group (USA) Inc.
375 Hudson Street, New York, New York 10014, USA

Penguin Group (Canada), 90 Eglinton Avenue East, Suite 700, Toronto, Ontario M4P 2Y3, Canada
(a division of Pearson Penguin Canada Inc.) • Penguin Books Ltd., 80 Strand, London WC2R 0RL,
England • Penguin Group Ireland, 25 St. Stephen's Green, Dublin 2, Ireland (a division of Penguin
Books Ltd.) • Penguin Group (Australia), 250 Camberwell Road, Camberwell, Victoria 3124, Australia
(a division of Pearson Australia Group Pty. Ltd.) • Penguin Books India Pvt. Ltd., 11 Community
Centre, Panchsheel Park, New Delhi—110 017, India • Penguin Group (NZ), 67 Apollo Drive,
Rosedale, Auckland 0632, New Zealand (a division of Pearson New Zealand Ltd.) • Penguin Books
(South Africa) (Pty.) Ltd., 24 Sturdee Avenue, Rosebank, Johannesburg 2196, South Africa

Penguin Books Ltd., Registered Offices: 80 Strand, London WC2R 0RL, England

SLOCUM AND THE MEDDLER

A Jove Book / published by arrangement with the author

PRINTING HISTORY
Jove edition / May 2012

Copyright © 2012 by Penguin Group (USA) Inc.
Cover illustration by Sergio Giovine.

ISBN: 978-0-515-15068-1

JOVE®
Jove Books are published by The Berkley Publishing Group,
a division of Penguin Group (USA) Inc.,
375 Hudson Street, New York, New York 10014.
JOVE® is a registered trademark of Penguin Group (USA) Inc.
The "J" design is a trademark of Penguin Group (USA) Inc.

PRINTED IN THE UNITED STATES OF AMERICA

10 9 8 7 6 5 4 3 2 1

ALWAYS LEARNING   **PEARSON**

1

John Slocum moaned in his sleep, turned on his side, and tried to shut out the noise from down the street by putting his arm over his ear. The hotel was worse than sleeping in the livery stable in a stall next to his horse. He knew the horse's night sounds and slept through them on the trail. But in Abilene, every drunk cowboy from miles around had come to town this Saturday night intent on whooping it up.

Uproarious laughter followed a single gunshot. He thought he heard the shouted desire to buy everyone a drink. For two cents, he would leave his nice soft bed and go get the whiskey, then strangle the cowboy who had disturbed him.

Rolling to his other side, he heard even more noise. This came from the lobby below. Getting a room on the second floor hadn't dampened any of the noise that he had expected in this Texas cattle town.

Then the door to his room burst open. The doorjamb flew into splinters and the glass doorknob hit the back wall so hard it exploded like a small bomb.

"You son of a bitch!" The hoarse voice was accompanied

by a sound Slocum only half heard in his sleepy daze—but it was one he reacted to instantly. He jerked hard and rolled off the bed just as the hammer of the cocked six-shooter crashed down. The echo of the metallic click was drowned out by the gunshot's sharp report and the sound of the pitcher on the night stand blasting apart into a million sharp fragments.

Slocum kept rolling, groped about, and found the thunder mug. It sloshed as he backhanded it through the air to smash into the cowboy's chest. A second shot went wild as the gunman stumbled backward to crash into the opposite hall wall.

Wasting no time, Slocum kept rolling, came up, and grabbed for his six-shooter in the holster hanging at the foot of the bed. He slipped in the slop from the chamber pot and flopped facedown. A third shot rang out, and he was sure he was a goner.

But no pain drove through him. He skidded around and finally came to his knees, pistol thrust out in front of him, and pointed in the direction of the door. His target had vanished. Then he lowered his gaze and saw the man lying in a boneless pile in the hall.

"What the hell's goin' on? You drop that iron, mister, you drop it, or I swear, you're a dead man!"

Slocum looked away from the corpse and saw another man in the hall, this one with a sawed-off shotgun leveled at him. There wasn't any way he could get off a shot and not die, blasted into bloody chunks as the man's finger jerked back on the double triggers.

"Drop it, you no account! I'm Marshal Wilson and you're one sorry, dead ass if you don't drop it!"

Slocum heard the hysteria in the lawman's voice. To resist would be to die. Even if he did as he was ordered, he might get shot out of panic and fear. He saw no hope shooting it out, and only a small chance to live if he put down his Colt Navy.

"I'm laying it on the floor," Slocum called, loud enough to cut through the marshal's panic. "No need to get antsy with that scattergun."

"Y-You slide on back, away from the gun."

Slocum did as he was ordered. The marshal stepped forward, lost his footing in the shit on the floor, and sat down hard. For an instant Slocum thought he was a goner. The marshal discharged one barrel, but his precipitous fall had caused the sawed-off shotgun to point toward the bed. Instead of Slocum's brains blown everywhere, the feather pillow exploded and sent a cascade of white fluff floating in the air.

"Stay, you stay put! You f-freeze!"

Slocum didn't move a muscle. In spite of the danger that remained—a single barrel at this range would cut him in half—he couldn't help grinning at the sight of the marshal all covered in brown slop and floundering about as if he were trying to ice-skate for the first time. When the lawman tried to stand and fell back, Slocum burst out laughing.

"You need a hand, Marshal?"

Wilson used the wall to steady himself as he got to his feet.

"Not from the likes of you."

"What's going on?"

"You're under arrest!"

"What for?" Slocum's laughter turned to cold anger. "He kicked in my door and tried to gun me down in my sleep."

"You murdered him!"

Before Slocum could say another word, the marshal grabbed the Colt Navy off the floor and shoved it into its holster, then slung the gun belt over his shoulder. Motioning with the short-barreled shotgun, he indicated that Slocum was to precede him from the room. He bent to put on his boots but the marshal stopped him.

"J-Just the way you are. To jail! N-Now!"

The panic was returning, warning Slocum not to push

the man any further. Dressed only in his long johns, he went barefoot down the stairs. A dozen men had gathered in the lobby to silently watch the spectacle.

"Hands in the air!" the marshal barked. He played to the citizens of Abilene now, more sure of himself. And that made Slocum even less sure what was going on.

Outside they were greeted with jeers, as many directed toward the marshal as at Slocum.

"Shitty job, ain't it, Willie? You sorry you left the range fer this?"

The comment provoked laughter and even more ribald jokes from the cowboys at the marshal's expense, but Slocum was aware of the undercurrent of whispering as marshal and prisoner paraded through the town. It was as if an invisible telegraph line told everyone what had happened. More cowboys poured from the saloons. Some threw rocks. Others spat. Slocum had the feeling the contempt for the marshal had changed to hatred for his prisoner.

What had he done? There hadn't been a chance to even defend himself against a murderous sneak attack.

He walked down the middle of the street, fights in saloons on either side of the street ignored by the lawman in his single-minded march of his prisoner to the jail down a side street on the east side of town.

"Get your ass inside," Wilson said, shoving Slocum. He jerked back and hefted the shotgun when he saw the look on Slocum's face. Eyes colder and harder than emeralds warned the marshal he had overstepped his bounds. He might hold the shotgun but Slocum wasn't the sort to push around. "In," the marshal said in a less assured tone.

The jail was larger than most Slocum had seen. It made sense that a town like Abilene would require enough cells to load up with drunks. Four of the six cells were already filled. One held a solitary prisoner, and Slocum was put into the remaining cage by himself.

"You somethin' special gettin' yer very own cell while

the rest of us gotta bunk together?" called a drunk from the cell across the small corridor. Then he held his nose and turned away. "Reckon Willie's doin' us a favor, puttin' that one all by his lonesome."

This caused a new round of jokes.

The man in the other solitary cell joined in. "You caught robbin' an outhouse?"

"Falling into an outhouse'd be an improvement to being in Abilene," Slocum said. He dropped onto the hard bunk and considered stripping off his long johns. Sitting naked couldn't cause any more derision than he was getting, but the drunken cowboys and their jokes didn't mean anything to him compared to figuring out what was going on. He had been sleeping, poorly to be sure, but minding his own business, and he hadn't even gone to a cathouse to find a female companion. It might have been better if he had.

"You hush up," the marshal called. He dropped Slocum's six-shooter on the desk and then collapsed tiredly into his desk chair. "I got you dead to rights. You shot Macauley in the back."

"Mac? This son of a bitch shot Mac?" This caused the other cowboys to come out of their whiskey stupors and rattle the bars, wanting to get at Slocum. Macauley must have been popular.

Slocum wondered what it would take to kill the lot of them. The way he felt right now, he could take them all with his bare hands, one by one or all at once.

"I don't want no more noise out of any of you, Seth. Mac might have been your friend, but this varmint gets a fair trial. That's what the law says, at any rate."

Marshal Wilson ran his fingers over the ebony handle of Slocum's Colt Navy, then couldn't help himself. He drew the weapon and held it up, aimed it at Slocum, and mouthed a silent *bang*!

Then he frowned, lowered the six-gun, and took a whiff of the muzzle. Frowning harder, he broke it open and looked at the six loaded chambers. Still not satisfied, he swung around and peered down the barrel at a bright flame in the coal oil lamp. Only then did he put the gun onto his desk and speak.

"I'll be hornswoggled. This gun ain't been fired."

"Hard to shoot a man when the gun's not been fired, isn't it, Marshal?" Slocum tried not to hope the lawman would realize what all this meant about his innocence, but the spark burned nevertheless. Proof was proof.

"Then who shot Macauley?"

"You're the law. Your job's to find out."

"I got to be sure." Marshal Wilson got to his feet, looked uncertainly at Slocum, then left. The other prisoners kept up their jeers, but Slocum settled down. The lawman was on the right trail. All he had to do was follow it to find who had really shot Macauley.

Marshal Wilson returned in about an hour, shaking his head.

"I'm lettin' you go," he told Slocum, working the key in the cell lock. The metallic click could hardly be heard over the protests from the others in the jail.

"You boys shut up and listen. This man's gun wasn't fired, but Mac took one in the back. Somebody outside the room shot him. Since this varmint's gun ain't been fired and he was in the room, that means he's not the killer."

The door swung open on well-oiled hinges, and Slocum wasted no time leaving. He had been in his share of cells and hated being locked up.

"Who killed him?" Slocum asked bluntly.

"Don't know. Doc Dawes confirmed what I had seen. Macauley was shot in the back, maybe from some distance away. From what I can reckon, the killer was at the far end of the hallway, then ducked down the back stairs."

"Maybe it was somebody down in the lobby. That was quite a crowd."

"They all came with me."

Slocum picked up his six-shooter. Wilson tensed but said nothing as Slocum strapped it around his waist. He knew he looked silly wearing a gun belt over his long johns, but he didn't care. Any man mouthing off was likely to get filled with lead—and this attitude showed plainly in his demeanor.

Slocum started to leave, then stopped and asked, "Why'd you go to the hotel at all?"

"Heard that Mac was on the warpath, goin' after a man who'd had his way with his wife. Damn, I got to tell Martha her husband's dead. Everyone figgered he'd die on the range, during a trail drive or maybe bit by a rattler. You know, the usual ways. He was a mellow sort. Dyin' in a gunfight wasn't ever thought of as a way of cashin' in his chips."

"Who told you Macauley was after me?"

"Not after you, not you in particular. Just somebody, like I said." Wilson looked uneasy to repeat that the cowboy thought his wife was cheating on him. There wasn't much easy for the marshal in this town.

"So he wasn't just drunk and looking to shoot somebody?" Slocum had already gotten that much out of what the man said after he kicked in the door. "Why'd he single out me? Or did he get the wrong room?"

"Could have, but Mac could read and cipher. His ma taught him as a wee one so he could read Scripture from the age of six. Think she intended for him to be a preacher."

"He's gone to meet his maker," Slocum said. "I intend to find out why."

"Now, don't you go rilin' them boys up. They were all friends of his."

"Then they'll be inclined to help me find who gunned him down. It sounds like an ambush to me. Doesn't it to you, Marshal?"

"A-Ambush?"

"Somebody told him his wife's lover was in that room and didn't much care who was there because he was waiting at the far end of the hall to cut Macauley down."

"Who'd do a thing like that?" Wilson frowned.

Slocum didn't bother pointing out that this was the lawman's job to figure out. He left a quiet jailhouse. The sobering cowboys had heard everything. At least the men in the calaboose knew he wasn't the man who had killed their friend.

As he stalked back to the hotel, he kept a sharp eye out for anyone inclined to challenge him. He was in no mood to bandy words. Lead would fly instead. But he reached the hotel and went up the steep stairs to the second floor. Where the room clerk had gotten off to, since he wasn't at the desk, Slocum couldn't say, but the door hung on one hinge. He grabbed his gear and left. The smell of gunpowder still hung in the air.

Rather than go back to the lobby, Slocum went down the long narrow corridor thinking how much it looked like a cattle chute in a slaughterhouse. He found the door leading to the back stairway ajar. That meant nothing since the lock was broken. Peering closely at it, he saw this was recent damage. But he still didn't know anything he hadn't guessed. The gunman could have come here, waited, and then shot Macauley as he stood in the doorway of Slocum's room. If the cowboy had turned slightly and presented his back, that would explain the direction of the entry wound.

Slocum went back down the corridor to the lobby and spun the ledger around. Everyone who had signed into the hotel had put a hometown next to their name. They might have lied, but they all seemed to be traveling through on their way elsewhere. None was a likely suspect to be cheating with the cowboy's wife, not from New Orleans, Baton Rouge, and a couple small towns in the East Texas piney woods.

He knew this didn't mean much. Macauley's missus might have carried on with her lover and then moved away— or the lover might have been returning after a trip. Slocum would have to do some serious asking to get answers to his questions. Unless he wanted to kick in doors the way the cowboy had, now wasn't the time. His nose wrinkled as he caught the effluvia from his long johns. He wasn't going to get anyone to talk to him stinking to high heaven.

As he turned to go, the clerk came in from the street. The young man froze in his tracks, eyes wide.

"Never said you did, mister. Really. He just took it into his head to—"

"The others upstairs. Did Macauley know any of them? Were they family friends? Of him or his wife?"

"His wife? Can't rightly say, but the other guests are all strangers. Never seen 'em before today."

"You lived in Abilene long?"

"Most all my life. Like Mac and his missus. She's ugly as a mud fence, but one of the nicest ladies you'd ever want to meet. Real religious, too."

"You never saw any of the men staying here before?"

"Not even you, mister. My pa owned the hotel 'fore me, so I seen folks come and go all the time for nigh on fifteen years. We come here 'fore Abilene was much more than a widening in the road."

"And you've never seen any of the others staying here tonight?"

"Never have. Said that."

This didn't prove Macauley or his wife didn't know the travelers, but it made the mystery even deeper. Slocum nodded once, saw how the clerk hastily made way to let him leave, then stepped into the street. Hot dry air blew from West Texas and caused him to stink even more. He decided on first things first and headed for the barbershop.

It was hardly four in the morning, and the barbershop was closed. Slocum didn't care since his need was so great. He rattled the latch until it finally fell open. Inside, he went directly to the rear of the shop and found the large galvanized tub behind a drawn curtain. After firing up the stove and boiling water for the bath, he stripped off his filthy long johns and dropped into the hot water.

He submerged until he couldn't hold his breath any longer and then lounged back to let the hot water lap around him. As he reached for a brush and soap, he saw a dark, indistinct figure looking through the front window at him. Then the shadow disappeared fast, making Slocum wonder if he had seen anything at all. At the moment he had more important things to do than worry someone was going to tell Marshal Wilson he had busted into the barbershop. After all, he'd left money on the counter to pay for his bath.

He almost wished the marshal would come running. He needed someone to scrub his back.

Slocum began the tedious task of bathing. Once clean, he could find out what had sent Macauley on the wild-goose chase that had ended with him getting murdered.

2

Slocum's clothes hung wet and limp on him as he stepped out into the morning sun. Its heat felt good against his face. Just being on the right side of jail bars felt even better. But what rankled and turned his gut was a series of questions left unanswered from the night before. Why had the cowboy decided to pick that particular room to kick in the door and declare his eternal hatred for being cuckolded? Slocum had taken a long while to think on the matter as he soaked off the stink in the bath.

It was pure happenstance that Slocum was in the room. Macauley might have been told to go there, but it was all a ruse to gun him down. In spite of what everyone said, Macauley had a powerful enemy willing to set him up for the ambush. If Slocum hadn't cut him down, then the cowardly bullet from the end of the corridor would do the trick.

As he walked, the hot dry Texas wind sucked up the water from his body and clothing until they were plastered and baked on his hide. He ignored that. More times than not, his clothes were filthy. Now he had rinsed them out in

11

the used bath water and had added a drop or two of violet from the barber's station. Slocum rubbed his hand over his stubbly chin and knew he needed a shave, too. That could wait. If he figured out who had murdered Macauley, he would treat himself to a shave so he would look presentable at the hanging.

By the time he reached the first saloon, Slocum was less sure of what his intentions were. He had been used and that rankled, but the smart thing to do was get on his horse and ride. There were a half-dozen ranches in the area where he could get a job as a cowboy, though not likely to be the one where Macauley had worked. That trail crew sounded as if they were a tight outfit and wouldn't take kindly to anyone having anything to do with their friend's death.

"Mister, mister, buy me a drink." A hunched-over man waved to Slocum. "I got a powerful thirst."

"Mighty early in the morning," Slocum said.

"What else I got to do?" The man held out a bent, broken right leg. "Yeah, I got stomped on by a horse. I kin face a man and kick him in the ass, 'cept I kin hardly pick up the leg with both hands." He demonstrated. Using both hands to grip his jeans, he tugged. The foot barely scooted along the boardwalk. A slight stumble and he had to brace himself against the saloon wall. Slocum wasn't sure which was more likely to fall down. The man was wobbly, but the saloon wall sorely needed repair. A dozen bullet holes had weakened the structure.

"There must be plenty of work in a town like Abilene," Slocum said. "You can push a broom."

"Merchants don't like me none. They think I'd steal 'cuz I look like this."

From the way he cocked his head to one side and looked suddenly crafty, Slocum knew he was lying. And that bothered him. The man was obviously lying and making certain Slocum realized it.

"Nobody gets anything for free in this world," Slocum said.

"Wait, mister, wait. Might be I got somethin' to trade fer a shot or two of whiskey. Even the rotgut this son-of-a-bitch bartender calls whiskey is better 'n nuthin'."

"What?"

"You mean what would a cripple like old Herk have in his possession to trade with a fine, strapping young buck like you?"

Slocum started to walk away. He wanted none of the man's self-loathing or crude soft-soaping.

"I know who's responsible," Herk called.

Slocum stopped and looked over his shoulder. Herk seemed a tad desperate now. He rubbed his lips with a dirty sleeve as his eyes darted about like a trapped rat.

"Well?"

"Well, mister, come on into the saloon and buy me that drink and I'll tell you who sent Macauley to your room last night."

"Tell me now. Without the drink," Slocum said, reversing his course and standing next to Herk. The man cowered. Even with a good leg, he wouldn't have matched Slocum's six-foot height by close to eight inches. Bent over, he scarcely topped five feet. From where Slocum stood, he looked down on the man's bald spot. The shirt showed that Herk carried a pack or something else slung over both shoulders. Slocum had an instant vision of Herk struggling along, a knapsack loaded with his worldly belongings, walking about town. And for some reason he had fresh black ink smeared on his hands and sleeves as if he had rested his forearms on a newspaper fresh off the printing press.

Slocum still didn't feel sorry for him to the extent of buying a drink.

"Tell me," he repeated in a lower tone with a steel edge to it now.

"You don't mess around, do you? You rip a man's soul out and stomp on it."

"I can always ask real nice or not." Slocum slammed the palm of his left hand against the wall beside Herk's head so hard that nails popped free and rattled onto the boardwalk. The man's head lurched backward, and he almost toppled over.

"It was that tall drink of water, Jerome Finch. He was bangin' Mac's wife, and asked Mac to give her up. That set him off. Mac, I mean."

"How'd Macauley end up at my hotel door?"

Herk looked around furtively, then said, "They got friends what don't want to see nuthin' go awry 'tween the men. Rather 'n tell Mac where Finch was sittin' 'round playin' faro at a gambling emporium across town, they sent him over to your hotel."

"Why my room?"

Herk shrugged, and it was an ungainly movement that showed more than his leg was busted up.

"Who can say? Might have been the first number that came to mind."

"He was shot by someone hiding down the hall."

"They didn't reckon on that," Herk said. "Might be they thought nuthin' would happen. Mac would blow off some steam when he found it was the wrong guy or maybe the marshal would have locked him up 'til his hurt was past."

"Who'd gun him down?"

Herk looked even more uneasy. He shook his head, the bald pate catching sunlight now like a pink mirror.

"Finch?"

"I never said that! He knowed Mac was huntin' him, but he wouldn't kill another wrangler. Not like that. They wasn't partners but—"

"But Finch wanted Mac's wife bad enough to come sniffing around when he wasn't home. Might be Finch and the missus decided it was time to end one marriage and get on with their lives."

"Mister, you got an imagination, I'll hand you that. I never said none of that . . . no matter how close to the truth it might be."

"You reckon Finch heard that Macauley was heading to the hotel to have it out with him?"

"Abilene's a boomtown. We got cowboys comin' out the ass. Nuthin' gets said that isn't repeated a dozen times in the next five minutes."

Slocum knew how that worked. News was always at a premium. A newspaper brought in on the stage was read a dozen times over. A town like Abilene was likely to have a couple local newspapers, all feeding the citizens what they wanted to read most. Gossip served to keep cowboys interested between the times when there wasn't newsprint. He had worked for enough ranchers to understand how hard they worked to keep down the rumors and put their men to serious work so they wouldn't gossip like old hens at a quilting circle.

"So Macauley knew Finch was likely to take a shot at him?"

Herk shrugged his curious gesture.

"Who sent Macauley to the hotel?"

"I know what you're thinkin', mister. You see how it might work out if somebody sends Mac to the hotel, then tells Finch."

"Anybody else sniffing around Miz Macauley?"

"Most of them fellers would be, Mr. Slocum. She's a looker. Or so I'm told."

This didn't jibe with what he had heard from the hotel clerk about her being a homely woman. Still, many a man on the frontier found just about any woman attractive if she batted her eyelashes at him.

"She interested in more than one man in her bed?"

"At a time? Who's to say?" Herk laughed, then coughed up a black gob. He peered sideways at Slocum. "Please, I done tole you what I can. Buy me a drink. To make the pain go away fer a while."

Slocum tossed him a nickel.

"Get a beer. Whiskey will tear up your gut worse."

"Thanks," Herk said in a caustic tone.

Slocum felt a bit unclean at having even talked with the man. The gossipmongers among cowboys were bad for company morale, but those cadging drinks in exchange for bad news and rumors were worse.

He headed toward the marshal's office to see what more Wilson might add to the story Herk had related. Jerome Finch might have pulled the trigger and killed his fellow wrangler, but somebody had told Finch where his romantic opponent would be—and set up the entire ambush.

"Him!"

Slocum stopped and looked around to see what the furor was, then saw a half-dozen men pointing in his direction. A redheaded man pushed his dusty Stetson back on his head. The day wasn't too hot yet but sweat beaded his brow. As he pointed at Slocum, his hand shook. The words coming from his lips told the reason.

"Hang the varmint. He killed Mac!"

It was a terrible thing to lead a lynch mob—and even more terrible because Slocum knew who the red-haired cowboy was without ever having seen him before.

"You calling me out, Finch?"

Slocum turned, squared off, and pulled his coat back from the ebony butt of his Colt Navy. He stood perfectly still, but the sound of his own heart hammered in his ears. Eight men in the mob exceeded his best effort to shoot them all without reloading. That wasn't likely to be possible from the expressions on their faces. They were all het up and looking for blood.

For revenge.

"You know my name?"

"Jerome Finch. You're the man who wants Macauley's wife."

"What!" Finch spun and looked at the men in the mob on either side of him. He grabbed a noose and held it high so Slocum could see. "I don't know what your beef is, mister, but you stuck your nose where it don't belong. We're gonna do what the marshal oughta have done."

"You shot Macauley, not me. My pistol hadn't been fired. Can you say the same about yours, Finch?"

"How's he know who you are, Jerome?"

"He guessed!"

"I didn't have to guess. You're not denying you and Macauley's woman are—"

"You shut up. You shut that dirty mouth of yours. Martha's a God-fearing woman, and she'd never cheat on Mac, not with nobody."

"Except you, Finch. You and her can be together now that you murdered her husband."

"You lyin' skunk!" Finch roared and charged, swinging the noose in a figure-eight pattern in front of him.

Slocum had plenty of time to draw, but his aim was off as the rope snaked out of the cowboy's hand and rapped him on the knuckles of his gun hand. The shot went off target but still drew blood. Finch let out a roar and kept coming. A second shot hit the enraged cowboy in the leg, causing him to flop facedown in the dirt.

But the damage had been done. Slocum had taken too long stopping Finch. The other cowboys rushed forward and tackled him. Slocum fought, kicking out and raking one cowboy in the face with his spurs, but the human tide finally drowned him. One man sitting on each of his arms and another holding his legs forced him to subside and conserve his strength.

"You kilt Mac. We're gonna stretch yer neck good."

The sentiment was shared by the others, especially

Jerome Finch as he limped up, clutching his leg. Slocum had only grazed the cowboy's arm with his first shot but the second in the thigh was more serious.

Slocum wanted him to bleed to death fast.

"String 'im up," Finch said, his voice coming in harsh pants. "Mac was my best friend. I won't tolerate the way he talked lies about him."

"And about Martha and you," said another.

Slocum saw how slow Finch was to respond. That told him something was going on between the dead man's wife and this cowpuncher.

"He don't have no call bad-mouthin' her like he did."

Then Slocum wasn't so sure. The expression on Finch's face was hurt and anger, not guilt. He grabbed the lapels of Slocum's coat and pulled him to his feet. With a powerful tug, Finch brought their faces to within inches.

"The marshal don't have good sense at times. Him gettin' the shit kicked out of him by a cow done that to him when he was workin' with us, but he forgot how good Mac was to him after the accident. I'm not forgettin'."

"You didn't shoot Macauley, did you?"

Again Slocum was taken aback by Finch's expression. A guilty man would have given himself away, but Finch's anger looked righteous. He shook Slocum hard.

"I'd give my life for that man. He was like a brother to me—more. I hate my real brother. Mac was a good man, and you took him away with your cowardly bullet."

Seeing no reason to argue when the mood of the crowd was against him, Slocum let them shove him back and forth to vent some of their anger. Then they lashed his hands in front of him and steered him toward the edge of town.

"Git his horse. I won't want trash like him settin' on a good horse."

As his horse was brought from the stables, the rest of the lynch mob took Slocum to a cottonwood towering at the edge of the road leading into town.

"You have anything to say 'fore we end your miserable life?" Finch asked.

"There's more to this than either of us knows," Slocum said.

"Damn right," called the man bringing Slocum's horse. "I let ever'one in town know there's gonna be a hangin'."

Dozens of people flocked to see the execution. Slocum grunted as they hoisted him into the saddle. He winced as they dropped the rough hemp rope around his neck and cinched it down tightly.

"Not that way," Finch said, pushing away the man with the rope. "You want his damned neck to break, not for him to strangle to death."

"What's the difference?"

Finch didn't have any good answer but loosened the rope so Slocum could breathe a little easier. He slumped forward and held the pommel with his bound hands. Turning his head to the side, he saw a couple dozen men and a few women watching with real anticipation. This was the most excitement they'd had in Abilene for weeks. At the edge of the crowd Herk moved about. From the way he bobbed about, Slocum thought he was picking pockets.

Every now and then Herk stopped and whispered to a man, always producing great consternation. Slocum wondered what the crippled man was saying. And then he had more trouble on his hands than he could deal with.

"Give that horse's rump a swat. I want to see this varmint's heels kickin' in the air."

"I didn't kill Macauley," Slocum called out, stalling for time. He twisted around and groped at the saddle flap on his right side. His fingers slid across the horn handle of a small knife he hid there. When the horse began acting all skittish, he almost lost his balance. The rope pulled him upright, and his fingers missed the knife handle entirely.

"You were there, you were responsible," Finch said. "We're only carryin' out justice poor ole Willie won't."

Out of the corner of his eye he saw Marshal Wilson hurrying forward, the sawed-off double-barreled shotgun waving around like a flag in the wind. As fast as the marshal came, he would be too late.

Slocum heard a palm slap down hard on his horse's hindquarters, then the animal reared. The noose tightened and choked off his wind. Gagging, he blindly groped out, but there wasn't anything he could do to save himself.

3

Slocum's horse reared again, forcing him to contort his neck to keep from being pulled from the saddle, but when the horse dropped down with all four legs on the ground, it had moved back enough to give some slack in the noose. Fingers working frantically, Slocum found the hidden knife and pulled it out from under the saddle flap. Reaching up and slashing at the rope took but an instant. Then the horse decided to bolt.

Slocum dropped the knife and felt the noose jerk hard around his neck—then the few remaining strands he hadn't cut snapped from the pressure. Unbalanced, he twisted about and fell from the horse.

The roar of a shotgun firing drowned out the mob's angry cries at being thwarted.

"You git yerselves back. Away. I tell you, git away from him!" The shotgun blasted again.

Slocum pushed himself up and gagged. The noose was still tight around his throat.

"Wait a second, mister."

Slocum almost passed out as air rushed into his lungs

when the rope was pulled free. He got to his feet and stood behind Marshal Wilson, who menaced the crowd with an empty shotgun. The lawman didn't seem to remember he had fired both barrels. More important to Slocum's well-being, the crowd ignored that, too, and backed off.

"We need to string 'im up, Willie. He kilt Mac!"

"Hush up, Finch," the marshal said. He turned to Slocum and asked, "Kin you git yerself cut free?"

Slocum looked around and saw the small knife in the dirt. He fetched it and began clumsily working on his wrist bonds. The ropes finally yielded. He grunted as pain shot through his hands when circulation returned. Then he gripped the knife, ready to use it on Finch and any of the others.

"He shot us up, Willie. He ought to be locked up fer that."

"Might be a better case for self-defense," the marshal said. His hand began shaking. Slocum knew he had finally remembered that he faced an angry mob with an empty weapon.

"You let us string him up or—"

"Or what?" Slocum stepped around, the knife in his hand.

"You're not scarin' us, you son of a bitch. The marshal might have got your neck out of that noose now, but we'll find you. We'll make you pay!"

Slocum didn't bother winding up as he swung. His fist connected with the tip of Finch's chin and knocked the man backward. Two men in the crowd caught him. Otherwise, he would have fallen.

A moment of shock caused the crowd to fall silent. Slocum acted to retrieve his six-shooter. It felt better in his hand, but he didn't have enough rounds left to make much of a dent if the crowd decided to continue their necktie party. That didn't matter. He would kill enough of them, starting with Finch.

His attitude caused the crowd to hesitate. At the rear some onlookers began slipping away to return to their humdrum lives. The sun poked up higher in the cloudless sky, making everyone hot and increasingly miserable.

"You better collect your horse and ride on out," Wilson said. "Not sure how long I kin hold 'em at bay."

"Not very long at all with an empty shotgun," Slocum said. He slammed the Colt into his cross-draw holster and brandished the small knife that had saved his life. Throwing a knife this small was pointless, but Slocum couldn't restrain himself. He reared back, then released the blade. It cartwheeled twice through the air, a silver blur, and then ended up point first in the dirt between Finch's boots. The cowboy jumped back, causing more furor behind him.

"Get outta town and good riddance," Marshal Wilson muttered as Slocum spun and went to catch his horse. It had stopped to drink from a trough a few yards down the street.

He felt prickles up and down his spine, imagining Finch or the others drawing a bead on him. He never looked back as he snared his reins and swung into the saddle. The edge of town beckoned.

"You're not gettin' by with this! You can't kill my friend and not pay for it, you murderin' sidewinder!"

Finch waved his fist in the air as others took up the jeers.

Slocum couldn't leave Abilene fast enough.

He rode steadily for an hour, then left the trail, made his way through low hills, and doubled back to see if he had a posse on his tail. Waiting close to a half hour convinced him Finch hadn't bothered getting his friends together to bring their vengeance down on him. As he studied the empty, dusty road, he thought hard about what had happened in town. Not much of it made sense, but coincidence was possible. Slocum would never bet that way in a poker game, and life hardly showed coincidences, but they did happen.

Macauley just happened to kick in the wrong hotel door and somebody just happened to be in position to gun him down.

Slocum shook his head as he worked over what the crippled-up Herk had told him. Might be that gossip set the wheels spinning that ended up with Macauley dead and a rope around the wrong man's neck. He rubbed the burns on his throat and got mad all over again.

He took a swig from his canteen, rolled the tepid water in his mouth, and then spat to get rid of the trail dust. A second drink didn't satisfy his thirst but made traveling on more bearable.

Turning his horse's face, he returned to the double-rutted trail and the next town, whatever that was. When he took a break at midday, he began to feel a trifle uneasy. Rather than dig out food from his saddlebags that had to be cooked, he grabbed a piece of jerky and ate as he rode north off the road. It took an hour, but he found some elevation that suited his purpose. He dismounted, got his field glasses, and started a slow study of the horizon along his back trail. In less than a minute he saw a dust cloud not kicked up by the restless West Texas wind.

Sitting and bracing his elbows on his raised knees, he watched as the dust cloud came closer, then moved back toward the road he had left.

"Damn."

The riders took form. Jerome Finch rode at the head of five cowboys. Slocum recognized a couple of them. They hadn't taken Wilson's advice to let the matter drop.

"Now, why are you doing this?" Slocum asked the fitful breeze whirling over the desert. It made no sense to him that Finch kept after him. If all the cowboy wanted was Macauley's wife, he was better off letting Slocum ride away. He could play the big man who had run off the killer—or he could even lie about it to Martha Macauley and tell her he had killed the man who shot down her husband. Any way he played his hand, he stood tall in the widow's eyes.

The way Finch doggedly hunted him made Slocum think he was genuinely aggrieved over the death of a friend and wanted justice done. No matter that the marshal told Finch he had the wrong man. Slocum understood evening the score when it came to murdered friends.

Finch was better off letting the matter fade away if all he wanted was the widow woman. He would never rest if he wanted revenge for a friend's murder.

Slocum lifted the field glasses to watch as one of the riders found a small hint as to the direction Slocum had taken. They all dismounted and began searching the ground, looking for more signs. They found it. Finch pointed in the direction Slocum had ridden. It took only seconds for them to hurry on the trail.

Getting to his feet, Slocum tucked the field glasses back into his saddlebags and knew he had to show more skill than he had so far. He might use his Winchester to pick off the men one by one. Eventually they would either give up or all be dead. If he shot Finch first, that might end the pursuit.

But Slocum wasn't that kind of killer. The more he thought on it, the more he believed Finch was an honest man looking to avenge a friend's death. That wasn't the kind of man who deserved Slocum's deadly attention.

He rode farther north, found a rocky patch, cut across it, then endured the hottest part of the day to angle northwest before turning southwest. The trail he left might be followed—but he didn't think any of the men behind him were Apaches with Apache tracking skills. Using every trick he had ever learned and a couple he had thought up on his own, he eventually made his way westward.

It took him close to a week to find a small town along the main road from Abilene. The best he could tell, he had left Finch and his men wandering aimlessly out in the desert, following sidewinder tracks in the shifting sand dunes, hurrying after dust devils, and maybe even finding themselves so thirsty they had to give up the hunt.

Never once had he left spoor showing he was headed west. By now Finch might be scouring Palo Duro Canyon. Or he might have returned to the ranch where he worked and once more did useful work tending a herd. Slocum didn't much care which it was if Finch had given up on his vengeance.

He rode slowly into town. He hadn't bothered to decipher the name on a post a hundred yards behind him. The wood had splintered and the whitewash lettering had long since faded. All that mattered was being away from Abilene, Marshal Wilson, and the murderous Jerome Finch.

Back aching, he dismounted, stretched, and winced at the pain in his shoulders and legs. The town was so small, there were only a pair of saloons. He went to the nearest one. The smell of cigar smoke and stale beer blowing from inside was sweeter than any perfume to his nostrils. Climbing the steps, he paused in the doorway to let his eyes adjust to the dimness inside.

"Come on in," greeted the bartender. "What's your poison?"

"Looking for a cold beer and some food," Slocum said.

"You found the right place. The Horny Toad Saloon's got the best damn food this side of the Rio Grande. You want meat or you want beans?"

"Both," Slocum said. His belly rumbled at the thought of real food. He had lived off oatmeal and jerky for the past week, hardly taking time to eat so he could put the crookedest trail possible between him and Finch.

"And a beer, comin' right up. Set yourself down."

Slocum sank into a chair, moved it around so his back was to a wall, and looked at the other three customers. One had passed out. The other two bet each other which was the stupidest. The cowboy with the knife stabbing between his outstretched fingers won Slocum's bet. The cowboy yelped when he missed and stuck himself smack in the back of the hand, causing his friend to laugh in glee.

"They do that all the time," the barkeep said, putting a plate of beef and beans in front of Slocum along with a fork and a mug of foamy beer. "You should see the scars they got on their hands."

"Not much else to do in town?" Slocum guessed.

The barkeep laughed and walked away, giving Slocum all the answer he needed. Some towns existed for no other reason than the inhabitants forgot to leave. From what he could tell on his ride into this almost ghost town, ranching in the area was the sole livelihood. With the land as arid as it was, a rancher couldn't graze too many head of cattle on an acre and providing water was a constant problem.

Slocum forgot about water and fodder as he dived into his meal. The beer went down well, not in the least bitter. He drained the last of it and rocked back, ready to order another, when he saw a furtive shadow against the window. Twilight had cooled off the desert already and left behind long shadows.

He reached under the table and pulled out his six-gun.

The shadow moved back and forth outside, as if pacing, then vanished. The creak of boards in the doorway caused Slocum to swing his six-shooter around. If Jerome Finch stepped through the door, he was a dead man.

Slocum cursed under his breath when Herk stepped inside the saloon.

The mangled man spotted Slocum immediately and came over, his left leg dragging slightly.

"Didn't 'spect to see you, Mr. Slocum," Herk said. "You get around, but a man like you's got to, I reckon."

"How'd you get here?"

"Didn't walk, that's for certain sure," Herk said, laughing. It sounded more like a crow's call than anything human. "No, sir, I hitched a ride with a freighter. He was bringin' over food and durables, so's I kept him company. He muchly appreciated it, he did."

Slocum started to speak, then clamped his mouth shut and thought hard.

"What's wrong? You look like you got somethin' chewin' at yer gut."

"How'd you know my name?"

Herk straightened a little. His eyes widened and then returned to their normal squint.

"Why, I heard the marshal sayin' it back in Abilene."

"He never got my name, not by the time you called me by name the first time."

"You must be mistaken. I know I heard it after you left under such a cloud." Herk snickered. "That Finch is a caution, almost hangin' you the way he did. That would have covered his tracks real good. Nobody'd ever think he was the one what killed Macauley."

"So you say."

"Might be wrong. Wouldn't be the first time, but he's a conniver, that one."

"Do tell," Slocum said.

"You want another beer?" The barkeep directed the question at Slocum but scowled in Herk's direction.

"Do you? I could use somethin' to wet my whistle, too."

"Two beers," Slocum said. He pointed to the chair across the table from him. He leaned forward just a bit and slid his pistol back into his holster. He didn't see any evidence that Herk was dangerous. Not like that.

"Much obliged, Mr. Slocum. And that is your name, I know. I know 'cuz—" Herk bit off his explanation when the bartender returned with the beers. Only when he was out of earshot did the man continue. "I know that 'cuz you got big trouble doggin' your every step."

"Finch and the cowboys with him," Slocum said. He put on a poker face when Herk vehemently shook his head.

"Not them. They don't count. Finch is not gonna try comin' after you. He's got a job."

"And a new woman to keep happy," Slocum said.

"What? Yeah, that's right. He's got Mac's woman to tend now."

Slocum sipped at his beer and waited. Herk would get around to saying his piece eventually. He finally drained enough of his beer to lick his lips in noisy appreciation.

Then he leaned forward and said in a hoarse whisper, "You got a bounty hunter after you. You got to be careful, Mr. Slocum, or he'll run you to ground."

"There's no call for a bounty hunter to be after me," Slocum said in as level a voice as he could. Truth was, he had more than one wanted poster on his head. The one that had proven the hardest to ignore was for killing a federal judge. The carpetbagger judge had deserved the couple ounces of lead Slocum had given him, but the law didn't see it that way.

No matter that the judge had forged documents showing no taxes had been paid on Slocum's Stand during the war and that he wanted its prime pastureland for a stud farm. He and a hired gunman had ridden out to seize the land that had been in Slocum's family since it was deeded by King George II. The judge had gotten a bit of land, but not what he had expected. Slocum had buried him and the gunman by the springhouse, mounted, and ridden westward without so much as a backward look.

The judge had deserved his reward. But a different kind of reward had been put on Slocum's head. How had any bounty hunter come across that wanted poster and found him in West Texas? It hardly seemed possible.

It hardly seemed any more possible than a stranger kicking open his hotel room door, then getting gunned down in an ambush.

"You watch your step, that's all I'm sayin'," Herk said.

"Where did you hear that a bounty hunter was after me?"

"I got nuthin' better to do than sit in saloons and listen. All day long, all night long, ole Herk listens to what gents

have to say. Sometimes folks are good to me and buy a beer."
He hoisted his empty mug in silent salute to Slocum. When
it was obvious he wasn't going to say any more, Slocum gave
in to the extortion and had the barkeep bring another beer.

Herk drank with gusto, then smacked his lips.

"Yes, sir, I listen good. The bounty hunter come all the
way from El Paso and is after you."

Slocum started to ask how that was possible. He hadn't
been to El Paso in a couple years. There wasn't any way in
hell a bounty hunter could have picked up his trail there
since there just wasn't any trail to follow.

"He knows you real good. Said you was wanted for a
terrible crime."

"Everyone's wanted for something," Slocum said.

"Not like yours. Not for murder."

"You're getting what happened in Abilene confused
with . . ." Slocum's voice trailed off. There was no reason
to tell Herk anything. The man had collected his due in a
couple beers.

"Might be, might be," Herk said. "But mark my words.
You gotta watch your back, Mr. Slocum." With a crash, Herk
overturned his chair as he stood, then he limped from the
saloon, pausing at the door to smile and put a thumb alongside his nose in some message to Slocum.

Then he disappeared into the Texas night.

Slocum nursed his beer awhile longer, alert to every man
who came in. They all had the look of a drover. Not that
bounty hunters wore a uniform or carried a badge declaring
to the world their profession.

With a single gulp, Slocum finished his beer and went to
find a place to sleep for the night. Even if Herk was wrong
about a bounty hunter on his trail, there was no reason to
stay longer in this tired town than the morning sun. But
instead of going to El Paso, maybe San Antonio was more
hospitable.

He gathered the reins and led his tired horse toward the

town livery. He rapped on the door to the barn but got no response.

"Hello? Anybody here? I need to put up my horse for the night and maybe find a stall I can sleep in, too."

The bullet ripped a hole the size of his fist from the door just above his head. A second shot sent more splinters flying and John Slocum diving for cover.

4

A splinter cut Slocum's cheek. The loud report of the six-shooter filled his ears again as a new slug ripped past. He hit the ground, rolled, and came up with his own six-gun ready to fire. His finger pulled almost to the point of discharging a round when he paused.

"Stop shooting, dammit!" He lifted his pistol and centered the front sights between the woman's heaving breasts.

She held the six-shooter in both hands, but it still wobbled all around. If she'd had a better grip, she would have gunned him down with her first shot.

"I'm going to kill you!"

"Drop the gun, or I'll drop you!"

She turned and faced him squarely. Her blue eyes were wide and round and frightened. She sucked in one convulsive breath after another but looked as if she were on the point of passing out.

"Who are you?" The question confused her. "Why are you trying to shoot me in the back?"

"I—" She lowered the six-shooter and pushed back a strand of midnight black hair from her face. She was pale and distraught. "You're trying to stop me from shooting you."

Slocum somersaulted forward, rolled again, and smashed into her legs. Her hands went up in the air and her pistol flew away like a deadly metal bird. It discharged again when it hit the ground. She had cocked it for another shot. Rather than be content with disarming her, Slocum kept rolling, his momentum enough to bring him atop her, his knees pinning her shoulders to the ground. From this schoolboy's pin, he could look down into her face.

He had to admit his would-be killer was good looking. Cleaned up a mite, she'd be beautiful.

He told her so.

"What?" She fought hard enough to lift him a little off her, but he wasn't going to let her go. "I wish my aim had been better. You deserve to die!"

"I've never seen you before. If I had, I would have remembered." He pushed the veil of her black hair from her eyes. The deep blue eyes shot nothing but hatred for him. Try as he might, he could not remember having crossed her trail.

"Let me go."

"So you can try to kill me again?"

He read the answer in her expression. How someone so lovely could hate him so much was a question begging for an answer.

"What is it you think I've done?"

"You killed him!"

Slocum heaved a deep sigh. No matter how far he rode, he wasn't leaving Macauley's death behind him.

"I didn't shoot Macauley. The marshal said so." He wondered at her confused look. "You're not Martha Macauley?"

"I don't know who that is, but you must have been on a real killing spree if you don't know how many bodies you've left behind."

"What's your name?"

"Angelina Holman. And it was my husband you killed like a rabid dog."

Slocum rocked back, then let her up. He didn't understand any of this. Angelina Holman was a stranger, and he didn't know anyone named Holman.

She scrambled to her feet and looked around wildly.

"Don't go for your six-shooter," he said.

"You'll shoot me down? You'll kill me like you did Michael?"

"There's a big mistake, and you're making it. I don't know any Michael Holman, and I've never set eyes on you before. Why are you so intent to ventilate me?"

"You are a gunman. I can tell by that gun of yours. It . . . it's worn and you . . . you look like you know how to use it."

"I don't kill unless it's in self-defense," Slocum said. His flat statement stopped her in her tracks.

"The way you said it, I . . . I almost believe you."

"I just rode into town. I've been a week on the trail from Abilene." He didn't elaborate on why it took so long to make what should have been a two-day ride. "I had the same problem there. Men think I gunned down a friend. The marshal cleared me, but they don't believe him or me. If you've never heard of a man named Macauley, tell me what you do know."

Her eyes darted to the six-gun in the dirt, then back at him.

"If you're willing to just talk, you can pick up your gun," he said.

"You won't kill me and claim it was self-defense?"

He heaved a deep sigh.

"If I'd wanted, I could have wrung your neck and saved myself a bullet and the bother of cleaning my gun."

She hesitantly bent and gave him a nice view of her rump outlined by taut clothing. Angelina scooped up the pistol and swung it around, again pointing it at him. He saw her resolve fade when he made no move for his own six-shooter. She finally lowered it.

"My husband was murdered a couple days back. We own a small ranch northeast of here. I . . . I was in Abilene and was told you did it."

"Who told you?"

Angelina saw hardness come to him and hesitated. Then she pursed her lips and made her decision.

"He owns the general store. He gave me your description. Said he didn't know your name, but he was completely accurate telling me what you looked like. He said you were coming to Gantt and—"

"This is Gantt?" Slocum looked around the tiny town. Some noise came from the saloon, but otherwise the town was peaceable enough.

She nodded, then went on, saying, "He told me you were going to be here and that the law wasn't going to do anything about . . . about—"

"Your husband's murder," Slocum finished for her. She bobbed her head and lifted the pistol, but Slocum saw that she had forgotten she even held it.

"I couldn't think of anything else to do but take the law into my own hands. I was wrong. You ought to stand trial and—"

"I didn't shoot your husband. Why would I?"

Angelina opened her mouth, then clamped it shut. The trapped animal look returned and finally faded as she started thinking rather than reacting.

"Michael wasn't even robbed. I've never seen you before, and I doubt Michael had. You're not from these parts."

"Slocum," he said. "My name's John Slocum."

She shook her head again.

"Never heard him mention you."

Slocum was fed up. He had been accused of two murders and almost hanged. From what Angelina said, somebody in Abilene had passed around his description and lied about him. A man had damned little in the world, but his good name was one of those things that had to be protected. As easy as it might be to simply ride on and leave this Texas tornado of accusations behind him, Slocum felt his anger coming to a boil.

"We're going back to Abilene. You and me, tomorrow. I want to talk with the man who told you I killed your husband."

"Why would you do that?"

"I want to clear my name," Slocum said, "and you're going along because your husband's killer is still out there. I didn't murder any rancher, but somebody did."

"You're right." She held the pistol now as she might a baby, the long barrel cradled in the crook of her left arm. Angelina rocked to and fro. Slocum watched the play of emotions on her face, finally becoming set in determination. "If you're willing to help me find Michael's killer, I'll be eternally grateful. I can't pay you—"

"Not asking for money," Slocum said.

"What are you suggesting?" She turned suddenly wary.

"I need to tend my horse and get a night's sleep. Be here at daybreak, and we'll go back to Abilene and settle this once and for all."

"You're letting me go?"

Slocum touched the brim of his hat, then opened the now bullet-ridden door into the stables. The gunfire ought to have flushed a stable hand, but no one inside stirred. Slocum fetched his horse and led it inside, aware of Angelina watching his every move. As he turned to close the door, he saw that she had hightailed it.

As he curried his horse and then fed and watered it, he thought about everything that had happened to him since that night in the Abilene hotel. Too much lead had flown; two men had died. And there wasn't any end in sight.

Unless he put an end to it.

Slocum bedded down in the stall next to his horse. Somewhere after midnight a drunken stableman came in, singing at the top of his lungs and scaring the horses. He never saw Slocum, and Slocum didn't bother telling him his singing was lousy. Before the stableman passed out, Slocum was again asleep—dreaming of Angelina Holman.

When he stirred in the morning, he sneezed, wiped his nose, and then sat up and looked around. Standing in the mouth of the stall, Angelina stared down at him.

"You said daybreak. It's past that," she accused.

"Had my rest disturbed," Slocum said, jerking his thumb in the direction of the snoring stableman. He got to his feet, brushed himself off, and then saddled up, getting ready for the trail.

Once outside, Slocum mounted. Angelina was already on her mount, a chestnut mare that suited her well. Slocum's gelding snorted and jerked its head around, ready for another day on the trail. He let the horse have its head.

"It wants to return to Abilene," Angelina said, trotting up alongside. "Did you get the horse there?"

"I've had this one for more 'n three months. Got it off a Choctaw up in Indian Territory."

"You travel around a great deal then?"

Slocum didn't answer because he didn't want to think about it. Seldom did he spend more than a few weeks in any one place before moving on. He might stay a season if he had a job tending a herd. That notion had come to him as he rode past Fort Worth on his way west. The XIT might need hands, though the sprawling ranch had never been profitable. Other spreads throughout this part of Texas always courted veteran cowhands, and Slocum had done about everything in his day except riding along as chuck wagon cook. That was a skilled position. Feed the cowboys well and they would perform miracles with the herd.

Starve them or, worse, poison them, and the surly crew would let a herd stampede just for the hell of it.

"We came up from San Antone," Angelina said. "Close to four years ago, with fifty head of Herefords. Michael was good. We built the herd to more than a hundred and were making a decent living."

"He have enemies?"

"I suppose every man does. You do, don't you, Mr. Slocum?"

"More than my fair share, considering what I've been through since Abilene."

"Michael was a good man, but he never took guff off anyone. He punched the preacher once for telling him he was a sinful man and going to hell."

Slocum had to laugh. That sounded like something he would do.

"Bet he never went back," Slocum said.

"Oh, we did, but the preacher was mighty careful what he said after that."

Slocum had to laugh again. She was an easy woman to like, making it even easier to forget why they were riding back to Abilene. They talked all day, changing their horses' gait from gallop to canter to walk and back to put the most miles behind them, and kept riding into the dark until they crested a hill looking down into the cow town.

"We made good time," she said wistfully. Angelina looked over at him, but he had eyes only for the sprawling town. Answers could be found there if he asked the right people.

"We could camp here for the night and go on into town in the morning. We've pushed the horses mighty hard today," he said.

"No," she said slowly. "It's best if we get this matter resolved quickly. Are you going to be safe?"

"I can take care of myself."

"Oh, I know that," she said hastily. "I meant, you said they tried to hang you and all. What if they try again? You can't hope to fight an entire town and win repeatedly."

"It's the middle of the week. Finch and the others were cowboys for a nearby spread. They won't come to town for another few days. Marshal Wilson has no call to cross me."

They rode slowly, letting their tired horses rest. Abilene

threatened to swallow them up with its tall buildings and closed-in feel. Slocum realized he hadn't appreciated his time on the trail until now. Being able to see the horizon no matter which way he looked suited him just fine. A quick glance at Angelina made him wonder if the ride hadn't been even better because of her. In spite of her anger at her husband's death, she was a lovely, intelligent woman.

But the town closed in around him, dark and foreboding.

"There's the store," she said, pointing to Cantwell's Mercantile. A smallish man wearing an apron was moving the last of his displayed goods into the store, getting ready to close down for the night.

"Sir, sir!" Angelina called. She trotted over, kicked out a leg, and dropped to the ground from horseback. "You remember me?"

"Why, I surely do. You're that Miz Holman. How could I fergit such a pretty filly?"

Slocum dismounted and stood beside her so the man—he assumed this was the owner, Cantwell—got a good look at him. Cantwell glanced in his direction, then fixed his gaze on Angelina's beauty.

"Can you repeat what you told me about my husband's killer?"

"You ain't doin' anything foolish now, are you, Miz Holman? Goin' after a killer like him's suicidal." Cantwell picked up a broom and leaned against it, looking at her thoughtfully. He gave Slocum more than a once-over this time. "You fixin' on hirin' this man to avenge you? You better let the marshal handle it."

"Repeat the killer's description," Slocum said.

"Well, lemme see. He was tall. Close to six feet. Dark hair, lanky, moved like a mountain lion. Had cold eyes, green like emeralds and as hard. That's about all I remember."

Angelina looked at Slocum and started to speak. He shook his head, silencing her. They both knew that was an accurate description of him, but Cantwell showed no recognition that Slocum stood in front of him.

"How'd you happen to see him? When he shot Holman?"

"Oh, I didn't see him."

"How'd you come by the description?" Slocum demanded.

"Strange, real strange. A fellow come in to buy some terbakky, got to talking. Said he had seen a killing. I told him to pass it along to the marshal. He wanted to keep on riding, was just passin' through."

"So he described the killer, and you told Mrs. Holman?"

"Sorry if I misled you, ma'am, into thinkin' I saw anything important. It was just gossip." Cantwell pushed himself erect using the broom as a crutch. "You didn't go and do anything foolish, now did you?"

"I—"

"No, she didn't," Slocum cut in. "What did the man who told you all this look like?"

"Kinda ordinary, but he ain't around town no more. I seen him mount and head south. He paid me in silver dollars. Said they was burnin' a hole in his pocket."

"And he wanted to clear out fast," Slocum said.

Cantwell sucked on his teeth as he considered the matter, then agreed.

"Anything I can do for you, Miz Holman?"

"She's fine, thanks." Slocum took the woman by the elbow and steered her away from the store. When Cantwell was out of earshot, Slocum said, "It's like before. Somebody spread a rumor about me, and Macauley tried to kill me but got shot himself."

"Do you think the same person murdered Michael that killed this Macauley?"

Slocum didn't have an answer to that. They walked slowly down the street. From a saloon on his right came an angry cry, followed by a gunshot. Men spilled out into the street. Slocum put his arm around Angelina and steered her to the far side out of range of any errant shots fired by a drunk.

"You can't call me that!" screamed a man dressed like a bank teller.

"What the hell are you sayin', Clem? I never—"

The fight began in earnest, fists flying and the pair rolling about in the dust. Men poured from the saloon and ringed the fighters, jeering and betting, egging them on and making comments not fit for Angelina's ears.

"Come on," he said. They walked to the hotel, where Slocum stopped.

"What—"

"You take a room, then go on back to your ranch in the morning. There's no way of finding your husband's killer," he said.

"But Mr. Cantwell said he had ridden south!"

"The man who gave Cantwell my description rode south. There's nothing to say he had anything to do with your husband getting shot."

"Somebody killed Michael!"

"Things happen we can't always explain," Slocum said. "It might be hard, but you ought to accept that and get on with your life."

"No!"

Slocum turned his back to her and walked away, leading his horse. The sooner she stopped trying to avenge her husband, the sooner she could settle down again. Barely had he walked a dozen paces than he saw a shadow draped in deeper shadow dart away fast, feet pounding hard on the drum-like sun-baked ground. He thought he heard laughter but couldn't be sure.

It was definitely time for him to take the advice he had given Angelina and get on with his life.

5

Slocum hadn't gone twenty yards when he heard footsteps behind him, pounding hard. From the impact he knew who was coming. He turned to be grabbed by Angelina. She almost bowled him over, in spite of expecting her.

"Please, no, Mr. Slocum," she sobbed, burying her face in his chest. "I don't have anyone else."

"You were doing a mighty good job when you tracked me down."

"I'm so confused about all this. Michael did all the money and took care of the ranch. We were doing so well, and I don't know what to do now."

"You can't own the property so I'd say you don't have any choice but to sell it and move on. You have people somewhere else?"

She backed off but kept her palms pressed flat against his chest. She shook her head, a soft cloud of hair floating about her face. He reached out and pushed it away to reveal a vulnerable face. He saw tears welling in her bright blue eyes but knew that shouldn't keep him from riding on.

"There's been an offer, but it wasn't enough," she said in

a small voice. "And it is our ranch, mine and Michael's. I have to stay, and you have to help me."

Slocum hesitated, his mind racing. He felt as if someone had grabbed his heart and squeezed down hard.

"Somebody's lying about me," he said after some reflection. Looking around town, he knew any number of cowboys would be willing to string him up, no matter how the ineffectual marshal protested. Finch and his crew would be at the head of the line with a noose.

What ought to have been shrugged off as a mistake had taken on the proportions of a life-and-death situation.

Worse, somebody had told the merchant that he'd killed Michael Holman, giving a precise description. Something burning in Slocum's gut told him it was the same person who had shot down Macauley after sending him on an enraged mission to kill the man who was ready to run off with his wife.

"Your face changed," Angelina said in a small voice. "What does that mean? What are you going to do?"

"Help you," he said. "Whoever killed your husband likely has it in for me and is spreading rumors that I'm responsible."

"So, find who is saying all those terrible things and that's who killed Michael?"

Slocum couldn't say. Who died after a boulder was pushed down a hill toward a town couldn't be determined. The boulder did the killing, but it would never have started rolling if someone hadn't tipped it on its way. Slocum suspected he had to find the man with the lever rather than those with the smoking pistols.

"What are you going to do?"

"First, I need to bed down my horse. Yours, too." With a quick grab, he took the reins to her horse from her hands. He turned, but Angelina stayed close to him, her hip bumping into his as they walked down the middle of Abilene's main street. The uproar from the saloons somehow faded as Slocum looked over at the woman and became more attuned to her. She occasionally glanced his way. He couldn't help noticing how her breasts rose and fell a little faster, her breath coming in puffs as if she was straining to keep up. Angelina didn't show signs of being unable to match his pace, though.

The slight flush to her cheeks told him something more was happening. He felt himself getting harder as his imagination rode along trails that ought to be closed to him. Angelina was a new widow. She had tried to kill him because she thought he was the one who had killed Michael. And Slocum's jeans got even tighter.

She was a lovely woman, shapely, determined, smart. He couldn't remember enjoying a woman's company more than he had the time spent with her as they rode from the miserable little town west of Abilene. He had set a quick pace to reach Abilene in a single day instead of two on the road and settle the matter of Cantwell's accusation. Slocum wondered if he shouldn't have drawn out the trip, just a day or so.

"You walked past it," she said unexpectedly.

Slocum looked back and saw he had kept going past the livery stables. He laughed at his inattention.

"Mind's on other things," he said.

"Such as?" Angelina moved closer, her hand pressing into his chest again. "Your heart's beating a lot faster."

"Can't imagine why," he said. He swallowed as her hand worked down from his heart, to his flat belly, and then lower to press into his crotch.

"I can," she whispered. "Is there room at the stable for our horses—and us?"

He led the way to livery stable and opened the door. Half the stalls were full. He put their horses into adjacent stalls, but saw that the other empty ones hadn't been mucked.

"What are we going to do?" she asked.

"The stableman obviously enjoys his liquor. Too much to deal with his work."

"Because he's not here?"

Slocum silently pointed to a pile of empty pint bottles in the back corner.

"What can we do? Go back to the hotel?"

"I can't wait that long," he said, his arm circling her waist and pulling her close. She opened her mouth to protest. He kissed her, cutting off any words.

For a heartbeat, Angelina resisted. Then she melted into his arms, her soft body fitting nicely against his hard one. Their tongues dueled, dancing from mouth to mouth. They broke off the kiss, panting harshly now. Slocum continued to lavish kisses on her lips, her closed eyes, her cheek and neck, and up to her ear. She gasped when he thrust his tongue into her ear.

"Oh, yes, John, that is nice, but I want more. I want this."

He grunted as she grasped his crotch. Her fingers began massaging the hardness she found hidden behind the denim until he wanted to cry out—or worse, waste his arousal like a young buck.

"There," he said. "Up there."

"The loft?"

"There's got to be straw up there," he said, guiding her in the direction of a ladder leading upward.

He didn't have to urge her to begin climbing, but she stopped when she was three-quarters of the way up. She turned, her back to the ladder, and gripped the rails tightly as she lifted one leg and draped an ankle over his shoulder. He stepped forward and found himself under her skirt. Her leg pulled him closer. He found she had stopped climbing at exactly the right place so his face could nestle into the fragrant bush between her legs.

His lips lavished more kisses on her nether lips and then he began tonguing her slowly. Every lap produced a gasp of desire from her. When his tongue invaded her, she almost fell off the ladder. He had to reach up and keep his hands around her trim waist to prevent her from wavering.

"I never felt anything like this before," she sobbed out. "I'm on fire inside. I want more. Oh, oh!"

Her leg tightened even more around his neck and pressed his face hard into her intimate region. He began thrusting his tongue in and out and produced a new wave of shuddery sighs from her. When the last one died and she sagged, she put her hands on his shoulders and pushed herself back upright on the ladder. Her leg swung about, and she turned again to begin climbing.

Slocum followed her quickly, pressing his face into her rounded half-moons, kissing as she went up and tumbled into the loft.

"I never had anyone do that," she said, her breasts rising and falling. "I liked it!"

"What else would you like?" Slocum stood with his head bent slightly because of the low roof. He tossed aside his gun belt and opened his jeans. The last two buttons on the fly exploded from the pressure behind them.

"Oh," she said in a small voice. Her blue eyes fixed on his manhood.

"Do you want it?"

"Yes," she said in a voice almost too low to hear.

Angelina leaned back, propped herself up on her elbows, and slowly parted her legs. She said nothing. She didn't have to. As her skirt hiked up, Slocum saw where his mouth had been only minutes before.

He pulled down his jeans, dropped to his knees, and caught up the woman's legs, hands under her knees. With a swift pull, he put her flat on her back and got her legs up to his shoulders, opening her wantonly to his probing.

She gasped as he moved forward. The plum tip of his manhood brushed across her sex lips, parted them, and then sank deep within her using a single smooth thrust.

"Oh, oh, yes, John." She shuddered with him completely within her hot, moist tunnel.

Slocum was unable to answer. The sudden intrusion left

him breathless and robbed him of speech. For a moment, he held himself poised, her ankles on his shoulders, her legs pressed down into her chest. Then he released her and moved back, sliding away until he felt cool air chilling his lubricant-dampened shaft.

Her eyelids fluttered and her eyes came open, but she was unable to focus on him. Slocum felt a bit shaky himself. He stroked over the tops of her legs, then more slowly bent her double again, once more sinking far into her. He paused to relish the heat, the tightness, the way her inner muscles squeezed down rhythmically all around him. When he could no longer remain motionless, he withdrew slowly and once more rushed back. He kept up the pistoning, hard insertion, slow withdrawal, until he felt the fires building within his loins.

When Angelina cried out in release once more, he no longer controlled his movement. Animal lust overtook him, and he slammed in and pulled out faster, harder, until the fires spread from his crotch all the way to the tip of his manhood. The hot rush spilled into the woman's willing interior. His hips went wild for a moment and then he pulled away and finally slid limply from her clinging core.

"Oh, John," she said, reaching up and putting her hands on his forearms. She tried to hold him close, but he released her legs and then flopped into the hay beside her. "That was magnificent."

"You're magnificent," he said, a finger tracing along the line of her jaw, across her lips, and then up to her forehead to once more push aside her vagrant hair.

She turned and snuggled closer, clinging to him. Slocum held her until they both fell asleep.

Somewhere near dawn the stable door slammed hard. Slocum disengaged himself from the still sleeping Angelina and peered down from the loft to see a drunken man stagger to the nearest empty stall and fall into it. Slocum sneered at the sight. The empty stalls hadn't been mucked, and it didn't seem to bother the stableman.

"What's wrong, John?"

He felt fingers groping for his arm. Angelina sat up and pressed her cheek against his back. He heard her soft words.

"Do we have to go?"

"The owner showed up," he said.

"Oh, well," she said. The woman moved away from him, stood, and straightened her skirt. He had to look at her, taking in the way her shapely legs disappeared under her clothing, making her once more the staid ranch wife.

She saw his interest, gave him an impish grin, turned, and hiked her skirt like a coryphée doing a pirouette, giving him a quick look at her privates. As quickly as she spun, she stopped, letting the skirt swirl back down around her legs.

"Let's go." Slocum started to let Angelina go down the ladder first, then changed his mind and dropped down so he could look up as she descended. The attention made Angelina laugh in delight.

He caught her around the waist and lightly lowered her. She rewarded him with a quick kiss.

Slocum spun her around and stepped in front of her when two men threw open the stable door and stood silhouetted by the bright Texas sun.

"There you are," the bigger of the men said, stepping forward. Slocum shielded his eyes and got a better look at the hefty man.

He was well dressed and didn't have a six-shooter slung around his waist, but the taller, whipcord-thin man with him did. He rested his hand on the butt of his Smith & Wesson and stepped to one side so he could shoot around the other man.

"Mr. Ralston," Angelina said, "I didn't expect to see you here. Are you following me?"

"I want an answer, Miz Holman. Now."

Slocum saw that they knew each other, and it was not a particularly cordial friendship.

"This is the rancher who made the offer for my property."

"Land, cattle, all equipment," Ralston said. "It's a fair deal, and you ought to take it. I have the papers ready for you to sign over at the bank."

"It's an insulting offer!" Angelina pushed past Slocum and stood inches away from the rancher. "Our ranch is worth ten times as much."

"It's worth shit to you. Your cattle are scrawny, maybe even falling down with splenic fever. I can take care of all that."

"Mr. Ralston has the adjoining spread, and our cattle do not have Texas fever."

"Your cattle," he corrected. "Your husband is dead."

"He was murdered, and I'm not sure if you weren't responsible!"

Ralston reared back, as if to hit the woman. Slocum moved like a striking snake and caught the brawny wrist in an iron grip. Ralston shook a little with strain as he tried to pull free.

"Wait, Barnett," he said.

"That's a real good idea, Barnett," Slocum said. From the corner of his eye he saw the thin man going for his pistol.

"I can take him, Mr. Ralston."

Slocum squeezed harder on the captive wrist, causing Ralston to grunt in pain. His face turned a bit pale under his weathered skin, but he didn't say any more. Slocum released him.

"I won't sell," Angelina said.

"He your new stud?" Barnett asked. His hand hovered near his six-gun.

Slocum didn't bother with the taunt. He faced Ralston and said, "The lady doesn't want to accept your offer."

"Lady? That whore—"

Ralston didn't get any farther. Slocum drove a left jab into the man's belly. As he stepped away from the man while he collapsed to the stable floor, his right hand flashed to his Colt Navy. He had it cocked and aimed at Barnett before the man could clear leather.

For a heartbeat, they stood there frozen. Then Barnett moved his hand away from his gun.

"Get him out of here. He needs a shot of whiskey to clear his head," Slocum said.

Ralston looked up, gasping for breath and hatred in his eyes.

"I want that ranch, and I'm gonna get it."

"You'll get more of the same if you don't keep a civil tongue in your head," Slocum said.

Barnett helped his boss to his feet. They backed away, but Slocum called to them before they got outside.

"How'd you know where to find Mrs. Holman?"

"Word's all around town where she spent the night," Ralston said. He shook his fist at Slocum. "You're not getting away with meddling like this, Slocum. Mark my words!"

The rancher and his hired gunman left Slocum staring after them, frowning. Not only had someone told Ralston where to find them, the rancher knew his name.

6

"Oh, he makes me so mad!" Angelina stamped her foot and crossed her arms over her breasts. Her cheeks flushed and her lips pulled into a thin line as she glared at the empty doorway. "I will never sell to him! Never!"

"How'd he know we were here?" Slocum asked.

"What? Why, he said someone told him. He's such a disgusting man. Michael asked him early on for help, and he refused. Imagine that. We weren't any competition. Ralston runs a thousand head of cattle and his spread goes—"

Slocum wasn't listening. He went to the door and looked out into the morning sun. Abilene stirred, ready for another day of commerce. He didn't see either Ralston or his henchman.

"Is Barnett his foreman?"

"I suppose," Angelina said. "You're not paying attention, John. I'm telling you that—"

"How'd they knew we were here?" Slocum almost whispered the question to himself as he continued to study the street, hunting for anyone with more than a passing interest in him and Angelina. He didn't see anyone, and that bothered him.

Somebody had told Ralston where they were and had given the rancher Slocum's name. That kind of interest went far beyond causal gossip. It was the kind of rumor mongering that told Macauley a stranger was having his way with his wife and a distraught widow that he had killed her husband. Men were dying as a result of lies.

"Clever lies," he said, but he couldn't figure out what anyone had to gain. Finch might have killed Macauley for his wife, but Finch had been gambling at the time the cowboy was gunned down. Or had he? Time meant nothing to a gambler, and Finch could have sneaked out to cut down his supposed friend.

"I don't understand what you're saying." Angelina came closer and took his arm with both hands, pulling herself closer.

Slocum tried to put into words the uneasy feeling fluttering through his brain like wind-driven cobwebs and couldn't.

"I suppose you ought to get on back to your ranch. It's not good leaving chores untended," he said.

"You'll . . . you'll come out? Soon?"

He looked into her expressive eyes and read fear now. He had seen lust and desire and humor and intelligence, but this fear was the most potent. Angelina had no one but him to rely on now that her husband was dead. Slocum wasn't sure he wanted the responsibility she wanted him to shoulder.

"I want to talk to the marshal."

"About Michael?"

"That and other things," Slocum said. Marshal Wilson was about the only one in Abilene who wasn't gunning for him, and the marshal lacked the spine for that. It would be easier for the lawman if Slocum simply disappeared.

"Very well." She turned and stopped. "Should we pay for boarding our horses?"

The stable owner snored loudly in the first stall.

"He didn't do much for us," Slocum said, but he fished

out a greenback and let it flutter down to the sleeping man's chest.

He watched Angelina ride off after she gave him quick directions to the Circle H ranch. When she vanished, he mounted and rode slowly through town to the marshal's office. He considered riding on when he came to the jailhouse, then dismounted. If he argued with himself enough, he was sure he could find a reason to leave Angelina to her own troubles. But someone was doing his damnedest to put Slocum in his sights, and that made him mad.

The door opened to the dim interior. Wilson jerked upright. He had cradled his head on his crossed arms and had been asleep until Slocum disturbed him.

"You?" Wilson squinted. "Git yerself on inside and close the door. The light in my eyes is givin' me a headache."

Slocum dropped into the chair on the opposite side of the desk.

"Who killed Michael Holman?"

"How the hell should I know? That happened outside o' town. Not my jurisdiction."

"You bother to let the sheriff know? Or the Rangers?"

"Folks in these parts deal with their own woe," Wilson said. He shifted uneasily in the chair.

"Maybe Ralston gave you a few dollars to help deal with your woes?"

"What are you sayin', Slocum?"

"Who shot Holman?"

"There was bad blood 'tween him and Ralston, that's for certain," Wilson said. "Ever'body knows that, but that don't make Mr. Ralston a killer."

"He doesn't seem the sort to do his own dirty work," Slocum said. "You so much as go out to the Circle H to see where Holman died?"

"Naw, his missus brung the body into town. Buried him in the cemetery. Not much of a ceremony, but at least she had enough to keep him out of the potter's field." Wilson looked uneasy. "She might as well have planted him out on the prairie."

Slocum had seen the way Wilson looked guilty when he had accused him of being in Ralston's pay. Ralston's cowboys undoubtedly came to town and hurrahed it on occasion, making it necessary to bail them out of jail. Life was easier all around if he had a good relationship with the town marshal.

And Marshal Wilson liked nothing better than having an easy life, Slocum reflected.

"Any notion who might have shot him? Any idea at all?"

"I tole you 'fore, git on out of Abilene. The longer you stay, the more trouble's gonna come boilin' up. If it ain't Finch and the boys off the Crazy Water, it can be Ralston. It's obvious there's things you don't know squat about, and Michael Holman's killing's one of 'em."

Slocum said nothing as he left. He had taken a good look at the men locked up in the nearest cells. All snored loudly, sleeping off their drunk from the night before. It was the middle of the week so there were only a couple. He doubted any of them had eavesdropped on him and the marshal. Even if they had, they wouldn't know more than everyone in Abilene already seemed to.

As the hot sun fell on his face, Slocum paused, aware of someone standing behind him.

"You come to pay your respects to your hired hand?" Slocum asked.

"What are you saying, Slocum?"

"The marshal. You've got him bought and paid for, Ralston." He turned to see if the rancher had brought his foreman with him. He was alone.

"You got a bunch of loco thoughts," Ralston said. "I want to make sure you don't get into any more trouble because of them."

"You kill Holman? Or did you tell Barnett to do it?"

"I wish I had killed the son of a bitch. He was a rustler! He stole my cattle and ran the brands."

"You tell the marshal that?"

"I take care of my own property. I didn't kill Holman, but I would have shot him or strung him up for the thief he was if I'd ever caught him with my cows on his property."

"Why are you telling me this?"

"You and his widow seem tight. Get her to sell."

"Even if her cattle has Texas fever?"

"I'll take the risk of killing the whole damn herd. My cattle don't have the disease. And I can use the land since it gives better access to the river so I can water the whole herd."

"She won't listen to me."

"Make her," Ralston said, a sneer coming to his lips. "It can be worth your while. A little pillow talk about how hard it is on the prairie, how running a herd without any help isn't going to be easy on her. You can put the idea in her sweet little head."

Ralston stepped back when he saw Slocum's expression.

"You do it, or you'll both rue the day!"

The rancher stormed off, every footfall producing a small dust storm.

Slocum was fed up with Ralston's threats. All the rancher did was make threats he had no intention of carrying out. Still, Slocum had learned something from meeting Ralston. Whoever it was spreading the rumors, it wasn't likely to be the rancher. He was gruff, bluff, and grumbled a lot. All thunder without lightning.

Slocum considered riding out to the Holman ranch but decided to make another stop in the saloon. It was early, and he didn't expect anyone but the barkeep to be inside, getting ready for the afternoon crowd wanting a beer with their free sandwich. He saw one man seated at a table off to the side, nursing a beer. He went over and sat.

"You get around," he said to Herk.

"Might say the same about you, Mr. Slocum," the question-mark-shaped man said.

"What can you tell me about Michael Holman getting himself shot down?"

Herk's eyes widened in surprise.

"Now what do ya want to know a thing like that for? Didn't know him, not personal like I do a lot of these gents. He was a rancher."

The way he said this turned Slocum wary. He motioned for the barkeep to bring him a beer, then signaled for two when Herk held up his empty mug. After the two frothy steins dropped to the table and Herk greedily sucked up his, there seemed less urgency.

"So?" Slocum asked, seeing that the man wasn't likely to say anything more without prodding.

"Don't like speakin' ill of the dead," Herk said. "When I'm planted in the ground, don't want nobody bad-mouthin' me."

"What's there to say about Holman?"

He leaned forward and said in a conspiratorial whisper, "I don't know this fer sure but heard that he was rustlin' cattle. That's what got Mr. Ralston all riled up."

"You think Ralston killed him for stealing his cattle?"

Herk shook his head, then said in the same low voice after looking around to be sure he wasn't overheard, "Mr. Ralston don't seem the type. Now he bribes the marshal and prob'ly the sheriff, this bein' the county seat of Taylor County and all. But the sheriff, he ain't never here in town. Heard tell he's got his'self a woman over east, over in Jones County, that requires his constant attention."

"Nothing gets past you, does it?"

Herk grinned, showing a broken tooth. Another had been capped in gold, now turned dull from too much chewing tobacco.

"I can't hardly git around, so I gotta keep my ears open. And my eyes. I watch."

Slocum started to ask about Cantwell, then found himself staring hard at Herk, who returned his gaze and tried to look innocent. Whatever else the man might be, innocent was as far from it as a pilgrim was from water in West Texas.

"Got to go," Slocum said.

"Where might that be?"

"Out of town," Slocum said.

Herk nodded, then ran his grimy, ink-stained finger around the rim of his empty beer mug, looked at what little remained in Slocum's, then snared it and downed the few drops in a big gulp.

Slocum laughed ruefully and left, going into the hot sun. This wasn't the time to be on the trail, but he had enough beer in his belly to make the ride seem easier. He mounted, then considered which way to go. A quick-moving shadow caught his attention. Something flitted into the alley alongside the saloon. By the time Slocum got his horse over to the alley, it was empty. On impulse, he stepped down and returned to the saloon door and peered in.

Herk still sat in the same place, running his finger around the rims of the beer mugs and then sampling the meager drops he captured.

Slocum glanced once more toward the alley and shook his head. Although he hadn't been out in the sun that long, he was beginning to hallucinate. He would have bet money that'd been Herk in the alley, but a cripple could never get in and out of the saloon fast enough. Mounting again, he rode east, not sure where he intended to go. What Herk had said about the sheriff made him wonder if there might not be some leverage applied to that lawman to get a decent investigation of Michael Holman's murder.

On impulse, Slocum turned off the road and went to the town cemetery on a lonely hill. It took the better part of ten minutes for him to find a fresh grave marked with a wood cross and Holman's name. He looked out over the prairie a spell, then decided. He had a nasty curiosity bump. Who killed Holman was chewing at him, but a bigger festering wound was the way Macauley had been gunned down because he'd been sent to the wrong hotel room.

Slocum didn't like being used that way, and he certainly found himself wrapped up in something bigger than a simple killing. Somebody had taken the trouble to pour lies into Cantwell's ear, giving Angelina Slocum's description.

Thought of the lovely dark-haired woman brought a new warmth to Slocum as he rode back to the main road. He counted himself lucky she was such a bad shot and even luckier that he had taken it upon himself to help her. The night in the stable had been something he would remember for a good long time.

He crossed the main road, then cut toward the northwest until he found the double-rutted road Angelina had said went past her ranch. The range was spotted with barbed wire fences. He suspected these parcels belonged to Ralston, but they might as well have been Michael Holman's doing since the purpose was to keep a cow on one side or the other.

The terrain became more rolling hills and occasionally green. Spring rain was often a stranger to this country, but this year there had been enough to give a fair cover of grass for the cattle. Several head per acre might graze comfortably.

As the road wound around, Slocum grew increasingly uneasy. The sensation of being watched warned him of danger. But a slow scan of the horizon revealed nothing. On impulse, he doubled back on his trail, then left the road and trotted in a large circle that brought him back to where he had felt the eyes on him. This sense had kept him alive during the war, and he still trusted it.

Somebody was watching him. Only he couldn't figure out who or from where.

When he saw a stand of post oak a quarter mile off the

road, he knew he had found a stock pond. His horse was thirsty, and he could do with a serious draft of water himself. As he found the trail and followed it, he got the overwhelming urge to turn and ride away.

He jerked to the side the instant he saw sunlight glinting off a rifle barrel. A split second later lead sang past his ear. Slocum threw his arms up in the air and tumbled from the saddle. He landed hard, moaned, rolled onto his side, and then waited. Every bone in his body aching, he waited. And waited. Not twitching a muscle, he waited.

Finally a man came toward him from the trees beside the stock pond, rifle pulled in snug to his shoulder, ready to fire again. He came closer. Slocum watched through half-lowered eyelids, acting only when he was sure of his shot.

He rolled onto his back. His Colt slid free, and he fanned off three quick shots at the rifleman.

Then all hell broke loose.

7

One of Slocum's bullets ripped through the brim of the man's floppy-brimmed hat, sending it flying. The light suddenly in the gunman's eyes did more than cause him to flinch. Slocum recognized Barnett. He tried to get off another shot, but Barnett began pumping the lever and shooting as fast as he could, sending death driving hard at Slocum until his rifle barrel had to melt from the rapid firing.

One slug creased Slocum's arm, sending a flash of pain all the way up into his shoulder. He tried to squeeze the Colt's trigger and found he had lost strength in his right hand. He tossed the six-shooter to his left hand. He was nowhere as good a shot with that hand and certainly couldn't fan off the remaining three rounds, but he was good enough to fire once and have his shot find a berth in Barnett's body.

Where the slug had injured the man, Slocum couldn't tell. He was more interested in swinging about, avoiding the wild fire still coming his way, and trying not to die. Barnett finally came up empty, but Slocum was in no position to make the killing shot. The six-gun hung down in his left hand. He flexed his right hand, then used his right forearm to brace the pistol. New pain joined that already in his right arm as the barrel burned through his coat sleeve.

"Give up, Barnett," he called after the running man. "I won't kill you if you give up!"

He heard a string of curses and knew this was all he was likely to hear from Ralston's henchman. Slocum shook his right hand and endured the pain long enough to know that he wasn't too seriously wounded. The bloody track on his arm was messier than it was dangerous, but the tingling in his hand told him Barnett's bullet had hit a nerve. He kept shaking his right arm until the tingles died away and feeling came back.

It was risky staying out in the open but he couldn't get to any cover—there wasn't any save for the trees where Barnett had run. Slocum clumsily reloaded, shook his right arm again, and then transferred his six-shooter back to his gun hand.

He could track Barnett, being cautious and taking advantage of what little cover there was between him and the stock pond.

Slocum put his head down and charged like a bull, giving voice to a roar that combined his fury and frustration. He burst through the ring of trees and looked around the small stock pond. Someone—Ralston?—had built up a dirt lip around a pond that might have already existed naturally. The water bubbled up from beneath the ground and gave added drinking water to the cattle and any passerby on the road.

When he reached the edge of the pond, Slocum dropped to one knee, used the dirt berm for protection, and carefully hunted for Barnett. The bushwhacker was nowhere to be seen. This made the hair on the back of Slocum's neck bristle. He had the feeling of being watched but couldn't locate the man anywhere.

He frowned when he realized he had experienced the same sensation in Abilene and along the trail out of town.

It hardly seemed likely Barnett had watched him all that time. If he'd intended to gun him down, he could have done so any time.

Sudden movement in the undergrowth across the pond sparked a reaction from Slocum. He stood and fired. The fingers on his right hand betrayed him. They let the pistol slip just a tiny bit and the shot went wide. The yelp he got in return of the lead he sent winging toward Barnett was more of surprise than pain.

He fired again into the brush where Barnett had dived. Nothing. Circling the pond, Slocum stayed alert for not only Barnett but any of Ralston's cowboys that might be with the foreman. When the brush rustled, Slocum started to fire, then held back. The brush shook again but he saw a rope around the stem. The rope vanished after a couple feet, but Slocum had the direction. Barnett had tied the rope there to rustle the leaves and draw Slocum's fire.

He drew fire, but not the way he expected. Slocum guessed where Barnett had to be hiding and filled that bit of under-growth full of lead. This time the cry he won from his accu-rate fire was one of pain. He had winged Barnett.

He wanted to kill him for the attempted dry gulching.

Then Slocum settled down to serious stalking. He'd kill Barnett if he had to. He'd prefer to see the man in jail, hat-ing every day of his incarceration, knowing Slocum was the one who put him there.

Slocum came to the brush where Barnett had crouched. The end of the rope was damp with fresh blood. He had winged the man, all right, hitting him in the arm from the look of the bloody fingerprints. A cruel smile came to Slo-cum's lips. He had done a better job of disabling his enemy than Barnett had. Slocum shook his right arm again, to be sure it responded and all traces of the tingling were gone before pushing on through the thorny undergrowth.

Here and there he found fresh blood. Then he heard a horse's hooves pounding away. Only long experience kept him from rushing forward after a fleeing killer. Barnett might have spooked his own horse to lure Slocum from cover. But as Slocum worked his way through the stand of trees, he knew that his caution was misplaced. Barnett had been astride the horse when it had galloped off.

He found tracks in the soft dirt and read them as easily as a schoolmarm read a primer. Barnett had run to his horse. Boot prints showed where he had mounted and the direction the horse had gone in a headlong rush to get away.

Slocum slid his pistol back into his holster and took a circuitous route back to the pond. He still had the feeling he was being watched, but it wasn't as strong now. At the pond, he cocked his head to one side and listened hard. It might have been the wind or his imagination but he thought he heard a receding horse—and it couldn't have been Barnett's. Making a careful circuit of the pond, he found a spot where a horse had been allowed to drink. Small boot prints showed where the rider had walked his horse forward. Slocum measured the distance and decided the rider couldn't have been more than five-foot-five. The stride was sure but not long.

Dropping to the ground, he examined one distinctive print in the soft dirt and found how the right boot heel was worn down on the inside. It didn't match the left. But pressure on the ball of the foot was even. He could only guess that the boot heel had fallen victim to a sharp rock or been partially shot off.

He took a break and splashed water on his face, then peeled back his coat and shirtsleeve to examine the wound from Barnett's rifle bullet. It had bled like a stuck pig but wasn't serious. The worst of it had come from the numbness in his gun hand. He thrust his hand into the pond and moved it around until the flesh turned downright cold. He pulled it out, held it up in the hot sun, and flexed all the fingers.

"Good as gold," he decided.

Then he hunted for his horse, which proved easy enough.

The gunfire had spooked his mount, but the lure of water in the pond was too great to simply run away. After a decent time, he pulled the thirsty horse away and mounted. He had a dry gulcher to catch. He rode after Barnett.

Slocum caught up to the fleeing man just before sundown. Barnett had been wounded more severely than Slocum thought, and his trail became meandering as he weakened. A stretch of prairie separated the two. Slocum drew out his Winchester and sighted along the barrel, but his finger never moved against the trigger. Instead, he thrust the rifle back into its scabbard and put his heels to his tired horse's flanks. To its credit, the gelding responded, and within fifteen minutes Slocum came up behind Barnett.

"I'm not going to kill you, though heaven knows I ought to," Slocum called. Barnett turned and tried to draw his six-shooter. He never got the weapon free. He fell from the saddle and hit the ground hard.

Remembering the trick he had used, Slocum circled and came up on the fallen man from an angle where he could see both his hands. From the spastic kicks, Barnett wasn't faking it, laying a trap for his foe. Slocum dropped to the ground and approached, still cautious.

He plucked the pistol from the man's holster and stepped back to stare down at him.

"Why'd you try to kill me?"

Barnett looked up, his lips moving but no sound coming out. Then he collapsed to the ground. Slocum edged forward and pressed his finger up under the man's nose and felt the slow gust of breath.

"Come on," Slocum said, grabbing a double handful of coat and pulling Barnett to his feet. The man tried to fight but was too close to exhaustion. He managed to take a few steps, and this was enough for Slocum to hoist him over his shoulder, turn, and then flop Barnett belly down over his horse.

It took a few minutes, but Slocum soon had Barnett lashed onto his horse as if he were a supply pack. The occasional groans as they rode back to Abilene told Slocum his prisoner was still alive, although barely so by the time he rode up in front of the jailhouse.

Marshal Wilson came out, saw who had come to visit, and then spat.

"Dang it, Slocum, you're a real bad penny. You jist keep on comin' back to bedevil me."

"Barnett, Ralston's foreman. He ambushed me on my way out to the Holman spread. We shot it out, and he came up the loser."

"He dead?"

Slocum let the marshal see for himself that Barnett was still alive, if barely. The two of them got the rope lashing off the man, and Slocum carried him into the hoosegow, depositing him in the first empty cell.

"You really want to prefer charges? He ain't likely to make it to sundown."

Slocum looked out the open door and saw that the sun was breaking on a new, sizzling hot Texas day.

"You got a doctor in town? Fetch him."

"Who's gonna pay for it? You?"

"He tried to kill me."

"Your word 'gainst his," Marshal Wilson said. "No way of knowin' what went on out there. The words you had with his boss sounded like you might be the one layin' the ambush."

"Ask him. He's awake again."

"Damnation," muttered Wilson, going to the cell. "You hear what Slocum there said 'bout what happened?"

"Git Mr. Ralston. Git him. I ain't sayin' nuthin' 'til I talk with him."

Wilson grumbled some more, then turned to Slocum and said, "You don't leave town 'til we git this squared away. I'll send one of those layabouts over at Clyde's store with word to Mr. Ralston."

"I'll be at the nearest saloon," Slocum said.

Wilson made a shooing motion. Slocum went directly to the saloon to get himself a shot of whiskey to ease the ache in his arm. For a crease it still hurt like hell.

Two shots of whiskey later he was feeling mellow enough to go out onto the boardwalk, find a chair, and sit to watch the traffic in the street. He saw Ralston coming in his direction.

"Didn't take long to find you," Slocum said.

"I was in town, no thanks to you. I had to talk to the banker about giving me a loan to buy the Holman ranch."

Slocum nodded. This was more promising, but he doubted Ralston willingly offered Angelina a dime more than he had to since he had low-balled his first offer to her, thinking she wanted nothing but to leave the ranch she and her husband had carved out of the harsh Texas land.

"Drop the charges, Slocum. I don't know that you didn't shoot first, but Barnett is a good man."

"Don't know about that. I do know he's a lousy shot or he would have left my carcass out there for the buzzards."

"Barnett looks after my interests," Ralston said.

"By killing Holman for you?"

"Holman was a goddamn rustler!"

"What's your proof?"

"Barnett told—" Ralston bit off the rest of the sentence. He glared at Slocum.

"Your foreman told you a neighboring rancher was stealing your cattle, and you swallowed the lie hook, line, and sinker."

"Barnett had no call to lie. Didn't put an extra dime in his pocket one way or the other."

Slocum thought for a moment, then said, "Might be that Barnett was rustling your cattle, making a few extra dollars off working for you."

"He wouldn't!"

"Might be true. Might also be true he was wrong about Holman."

"Just because you and that whore wife of Holman's—" Ralston clamped his mouth shut as Slocum pulled his six-shooter and cocked it.

"Keep a civil tongue in your head."

"You can't know what Michael Holman was like. You just blew into Abilene."

"There's something to what you say, but any man who had as devoted a wife as Angelina Holman, well, it's not likely he was the owlhoot you make him out to be."

"Burn in hell." Ralston stormed off.

Slocum returned his six-gun to its holster and considered going into the saloon for another drink. It was still early, but his arm ached something fierce. He stopped when he saw a huge man carrying a small black bag coming from the jailhouse.

"Doc!" he called. The man looked up, verifying Slocum's supposition. "You got a minute to patch me up?"

"It's one of those days, and it ain't even eight o'clock," the doctor grumbled.

He was a huge man, taller than Slocum's six feet by an inch or two. He carried his more than two hundred pounds lightly and moved with easy grace for such a big man.

"Let's see what's ailing you." The doctor saw the bloody sleeve and worked to open the catch on his bag. He rummaged about and came out with a roll of bandages and a bottle of carbolic acid.

Slocum bared his arm. The doctor ran his bear-paw hand over the arm with surprising gentleness and showed even more dexterity cleaning and bandaging the wound.

"You don't look it, but you've got the hands of a surgeon."

"Was, during the war. Ain't no grace required in most of that surgery." He closed his bag and said, "I could lop off an arm or leg inside a minute. Difference 'tween me and most of the others, my patients lived." He shook his head. "Not that they saw that as a boon, mind you. Can't say I don't agree in most cases. But you? Easy wound. That'll be fifty cents."

Slocum paid him.

"You patch up Barnett? Over at the jail?"

"Did. He'll make it. Didn't even have to whack off any important pieces." The doctor looked hard at Slocum. "You're the one that brought him in, aren't you? Willie's all upset over it since he had to cross Monty Ralston."

"I've met Mr. Ralston," Slocum said.

"I just bet you have." The doctor shook his head. "Things haven't been the same around here lately, not since that young fellow Holman was stabbed."

"Stabbed? I thought he was gunned down."

"Stabbed a couple times in the belly. Right about here," he said, drawing a line across his side just under his left rib. "One cut went up and into his heart. That 'bout killed him outright." He fumbled around in his bag and brought out an envelope. A couple quick taps caused something to come loose inside. He held it open for Slocum to see.

"What is it?"

"Looks to me like the point of the knife that killed Holman. It was broke off and lodged in the muscle around his heart. Might have cracked when it bounced off a rib, then fractured as it killed him."

"Why'd you keep it?"

The doctor shrugged, then said, "If Willie ever finds a knife with the point busted off, I might piece it back together. That'd mean whoever had the knife was likely the killer."

"You tell anyone about this?" Slocum tapped the envelope.

"Willie knows. Don't know that he'd tell anyone else."

"Let's go back to the jail. The marshal's got Barnett's gear."

"You think he done in that Holman boy?"

Slocum and the doctor walked back to find the marshal unsaddling Barnett's horse.

"I ain't ready fer you, Slocum. You ruined a perfectly fine day already."

"You're not the only one with that sentiment," Slocum said. "Is there a knife in Barnett's gear?"

Wilson looked hard at him, then at the doctor, who held up the envelope. Slocum thought the marshal turned a shade paler under his suntan and grime. He dropped the saddle and picked up saddlebags he'd already tossed inside the jail. Wilson brought the saddlebags out and upended them, spilling the contents to the ground at their feet. A short knife gleamed in the sun. He picked it up.

The point was broken off.

"Don't mean nuthin'," Wilson said. "Happens all the time to cheap knives like this."

The doctor fished out the broken tip. It fit perfectly onto the blade.

"Damnation," the marshal said again. "I'd never have thought it of Barnett. Never in a hundred years."

Slocum caught rapid movement from the corner of his eye, but when he turned, nothing was there. Again, nothing was there.

8

"I got the evidence," Marshal Wilson said testily. "Come clean and might be I won't see you get your damned neck stretched."

Barnett propped himself up in the jail cell, back against a cold stone wall, and stared at the lawman.

"You can't have proof. I didn't kill Holman!"

"Ralston wanted him dead, and you do what your boss asks," Slocum said. He got a hot, angry glare from the marshal. He ignored it. "With Holman dead, Ralston could buy his ranch for a song and a dance."

"Why'd he want to? He's got more cattle than any ten men need. And his danged ranch? It keeps going so far beyond the horizon your horse'd drop dead 'fore you got to the boundary."

"Water," Slocum said.

"I got the knife," Wilson cut in. "The tip of the knife blade was stuck inside Holman. Doc took it out and saved it. Fits yer knife perfect-like."

"I lost my knife. Haven't got a new one yet."

"This yours?" Wilson held up the knife.

"Not mine. Mine's got a horn handle. Horn from a buck I kilt up in Colorado when I was ramrod on a drive up to Wyoming."

"You sure?" Wilson held the knife through the bars, as if begging Barnett to grab it from him.

Slocum saw the hesitation, the evaluation of his chances, but Barnett never stirred. Whether he couldn't because of his wounds or because he knew there wasn't any chance he could get free, even with the weapon, was a question to be argued over for some time.

"I didn't kill Holman. I would have, but I didn't."

"You'll burn in hell for your crime, Barnett," the marshal said. He pulled the knife back through the bars and stalked off.

Slocum stared at the prisoner for a moment, then trailed Wilson outside into the hot sun.

"I knowed you was bad luck the instant I set eyes on you," Wilson said, almost spitting in anger. "Why didn't you keep ridin' like I told you to?"

"He didn't kill Holman," Slocum said.

"What?" Wilson squinted and finally said, "Yer not makin' sense, Slocum. You brung him in. We found the murder weapon. I wouldn't put it past you to frame him, but the doc? He's as honest a man as I ever did see. He wouldn't make up evidence."

"The knife was used to kill Holman. That's as sure a thing as can be," Slocum said. "But Barnett didn't use the knife."

"So who did, Mr. High-and-Mighty Know-It-All?"

Slocum didn't have an answer. As much as he wished Barnett were guilty, he had played enough poker with enough cowboys in his day to know when they had good hands and when they were bluffing. Barnett wasn't good enough an actor to conceal his guilt. When he denied the murder, he had been outraged at the accusation. If he had killed Holman, he was more likely to be arrogant about it and brag on the details.

That proved nothing, Slocum knew, but all the little things that would point to Barnett being the killer weren't there.

Slocum pushed back his coat to better get to his six-shooter when he saw Ralston storming along the street toward the jail. He wondered if the man ever walked anywhere or if he was always stomping and kicking up dust clouds.

"You've got my foreman locked up in there," Ralston said. "Let him go."

"Now, Mr. Ralston, it ain't as easy as that," Wilson started.

Ralston shoved the marshal back so hard, he hit the wall and his teeth rattled. But before the rancher could take another step, he found himself stopped with the cold steel muzzle of a Colt Navy shoved into his belly.

"Don't know how most places work, but they don't let anybody push around the town marshal," Slocum said.

"You're not a deputy. What's your part in this?" Ralston's belligerence didn't fade although Slocum could easily put a slug into his stomach. Point blank, the muzzle flash was as likely to set fire to his clothing and burn him to death as anything. Nothing deterred Monty Ralston.

"I can't say." Slocum's reply was an honest one. He had never wanted to stay in Abilene, yet circumstances kept piling up, forcing him to do that very thing.

"I got a herd to tend. I need Barnett. You hear, Willie? You let my man out of your lockup!"

Wilson dusted himself off. Slocum saw the conflict on the lawman's face. He was used to taking orders, but Ralston had overstepped his bounds when he shoved him. That had given Wilson some *cojones*.

"I got good evidence your boy kilt Holman. Looks like we'll be goin' to trial when the judge comes through."

"Judge? Trial? Barnett's not standing trial!"

"Don't make me run you in for disorderly conduct and

assaultin' a peace officer," Wilson said. "Nobody'd like it if you forced me to do that."

"Look, Willie, this is all a big misunderstanding. You know how riled I can get. I didn't mean to push you like that, but I did, and for that I apologize."

"Apology accepted."

"So let Barnett out and—"

"He stays put. 'Til the trial."

Slocum thought he would have to pull the trigger to stop Ralston as he lurched forward, hands groping for Wilson's throat. The rancher turned livid, so red in the face that the bulging vein on his temple looked ready to explode. At the last instant, Ralston checked his attack and backed off.

"You haven't heard the last of this."

Then he spun and stormed away, as mad as when he had come over to the jailhouse. Slocum wasn't sure who the rancher directed the threat toward. He slowly slid his pistol back into the cross-draw holster and watched the marshal's reaction to it all.

He had gone pale, but now his color was not only returning but giving a flush to his face. Anger built to the bursting point.

"Git the hell outta my sight, Slocum. You're the cause of all this. I don't know how or why, but you are."

"How do you figure, Marshal?"

"None of this was a problem 'fore you showed up in town."

Slocum didn't bother pointing out that Michael Holman had been killed prior to his arrival. Whatever had driven Macauley was before Slocum came to Abilene, too. With the marshal in such a poorly contained rage, facts meant nothing.

He followed Ralston, but he was too late to catch the man at the livery stable. He had ridden out, leaving the stableman in a snit because the rancher hadn't paid. Slocum considered his chances of learning anything if he rode down Ralston, then slowly walked back to the saloon near the jailhouse. There weren't any more customers inside than before.

But the one sitting at the same chair he had occupied before drew Slocum.

"You have your ear to the ground, Herk," he said. "Who else besides Ralston wants the Holman ranch?"

"Wants it? For what? It's the butt end of an ugly mule, that spread." Herk made a snorting noise, then pushed back and stood, using the table and chair back for support. When he got his balance, he went to the bar, one leg dragging behind. Slocum watched as Herk dragged the inside of his right heel along the floor, almost stumbling as he went. He ordered a beer, then came back. In spite of his uneven gait and his filled mug swaying to and fro, he managed to return without spilling a drop. He fell into the chair and used both hands to pull his gimpy leg around.

"Why else would someone kill Holman?" Slocum asked.

"Mighta got into a fight over his wife. You seen how purty she is. Purty enough for a man to kill for, a man what ain't seen another woman for a month whilst he was out on the range."

"You got a name to go with that guess?"

Herk looked all thoughtful, then said, "Could be the fellow they got locked up. The one you got locked up."

"Barnett?" This notion startled Slocum since he hadn't considered it.

"Him and Miz Holman mighta been foolin' 'round. Not sayin' they was, mind you, but could be all in Barnett's head. That man looked plumb loco to me."

Another thought struck Slocum, one that turned him cold as ice inside. He pushed back from the table and left without a word, Herk calling after him to wait. The barkeep was demanding Herk pay up for his beer, now that the likeliest source of money had dried up. Slocum ignored it all. What if the one sweet on Angelina wasn't Barnett but Monty Ralston?

Slocum rode like the wind toward the Holman ranch, his mind tumbling and stumbling over too many guesses. He needed certainty; he needed facts. He wasn't likely to get them until he talked again with Angelina and found if it was only her ranch that Ralston wanted. In spite of the need for reaching the ranch as fast as he could, his horse had been worn out on the trail and began to falter. As much as he wanted to press on, he knew his horse would either balk or just die under him if he tried to continue at the breakneck pace he had set.

Slowing to a walk, Slocum realized he had to give the horse more of a rest than this. He dismounted and walked alongside so the gelding wouldn't have to carry his weight for a mile or so. Footsore, Slocum mounted again and alternated a walk with a trot. He felt the pressure of time and circumstance weighing down on him, but there was nothing he could do.

After what seemed an eternity—and it well might have been since the sun was sinking on the distant horizon—he found the road leading to the Circle H and took it. By the time he got to the ranch house, apprehension had built to the point where he wanted to explode.

Chickens milled about in the yard between the house and barn, pecking at the ground, hunting for food. Hungry birds came toward him, but his horse kicked out and scattered them.

"Not fed, no light in the house," Slocum muttered to himself. He dismounted and drew his six-gun, not knowing what he would find inside.

Pulling back the latch string, he waited for any reaction from inside. Barreling in might win him a shotgun blast to the gut. After he had waited and not heard anything, he eased open the door. Pressing close to the doorjamb, he slipped inside, careful not to silhouette himself against the sinking sun.

The room was small but well kept. Moving like a shadow,

he found the bedroom. The bed hadn't been made and a washbasin on a side table was dry as a bone. Nobody had been here in a spell. He went back to the main room and poked through the larder. Not much in the way of food. And nothing had been prepared recently.

When he heard a soft sound, a crackling noise, he whirled about, gun aimed and ready to fire. A gray cat dropped down, ears flattened, and hissed at him. Then it silently left, taking care not to step again on the old newspaper that had alerted him. He tracked it with his six-gun until it faded tracelessly into the twilight.

It took another five minutes to assure himself that the house was empty. He went to the barn. If Angelina had come back, her horse would be in a stall. There were two dairy cows in stalls, but from the look of their udders, they hadn't been milked. They lowed in pain. Slocum didn't have time to tend them so he led them out and released them. There had to be a calf or two nearby that would relieve the pain—if the mama cows permitted it.

But Angelina's horse was not in the barn. He made a thorough examination of the stalls, then frowned. One had fresh horse flop in it. Her horse had been here, within the past few hours if he could tell.

Then he looked up and saw a white sheet of paper punched onto a nail at the front of the stall. Slocum took it and held it up. The penciled writing was too faint for him to read. He went to the back of the barn, found a lantern, and lit it. With the flickering yellow light sending crazy shadows over the page, Slocum slowly read the note.

Ralston had taken Angelina captive and wanted to trade Barnett for her.

9

"Well, I reckon that's possible," Marshal Wilson said, staring at the kidnap note on his desk. He scratched himself, then shook his head. "Don't like to hand over prisoners like that, though."

Slocum wanted Angelina released, but it galled him that Ralston had resorted to such an underhanded way of freeing his foreman. Angelina wasn't part of the problem, and as much as he thought Barnett was innocent of the Holman murder, he didn't want to see the marshal cave in to the demand. In the back of his mind he worked over the possibility that Ralston was sweet on Angelina and had murdered her husband. If that were the case, she was in the worst possible hands now.

Or the best. Would a man who felt unrequited love for a woman hurt her?

Slocum couldn't work any of it out to his satisfaction. Did Ralston think Barnett was that valuable as a foreman, or was there more to it? He knew powerful ranchers like Ralston felt they were above the law. And most were. From the way Wilson jumped whenever the rancher yelled "frog," that was true. At least it had been until Ralston had shoved him against the jailhouse wall. That had been a breaking point for the lawman, no matter how much money Ralston might give him under the table to look the other way when his boys came to town and shot it up. Ralston should never have publicly humiliated Wilson.

"Where's he likely to have taken her?" Slocum asked.

"If you're thinkin' on findin' her yourself, you might as well try pissin' up a rope. Ralston knows this land better 'n anybody. If he wanted to hide her, nobody'd find her."

Slocum left the marshal and went to Barnett's cell.

"You heard what your boss did."

"Cain't rightly believe he'd do that for me. When you lettin' me go?"

"Where would he take her?"

"Now, that wouldn't be smart for me to answer, would it? If I tell you, you rescue her, I rot in jail."

Slocum moved closer and lowered his voice so only Barnett could hear.

"If he harms one hair on her head, you won't live long enough to rot in jail."

"You cain't threaten me, Slocum!"

"It's a promise. I don't think you killed Holman, but I'm not so sure about your boss. He just might have."

"To get that pissy little ranch?" Barnett laughed, then spat into the corner of the cell. His aim this time was more accurate than it had been in the past. "Mr. Ralston is a man of what they call means. He's got more money than you could ever count. If you can even count."

"I don't mean the Holman ranch."

Barnett frowned, then said, "You cain't mean you think Mr. Ralston wants her? He kin get any woman he wants."

"Killing Michael Holman and not getting caught would prove that, wouldn't it?"

Barnett looked skeptical, but Slocum saw the calculation going on behind the man's watery eyes. Barnett might discount the idea, but there was enough truth in it that he couldn't be openly boastful one way or the other.

"If you want her, you'd better do whatever the boss says you ought to."

"All I've got in his note saying he kidnapped her."

"There'll be more then, won't there?" Barnett looked smug.

"One bullet is all it'll take so you don't give a rat's ass one way or the other," Slocum said, leaving the cell block before Barnett could retort.

"You shouldn't rile my prisoners," Wilson said. "It makes 'em mighty restless. Sometimes, they even throw their food around and make one whale of a mess."

"Barnett probably doesn't know where he would take her."

"We got to wait, then. What's the point in takin' her if he don't tell us how to make the exchange?"

Slocum looked out the open door into the street and saw Herk struggling along in the hot sun, his bad leg almost useless behind him. Once, he stepped on a rock in the street and fell to his knees. Painfully standing, he kept up his journey until he reached the jail.

"Marshal, got this!" Herk held up a sheet of paper. "One of Mr. Ralston's hands done brought it to me and said to be sure you got it." Herk looked at Slocum and said, "Didn't figure you'd be here."

"Why not?" Wilson asked. "He was the one what brung me the kidnap note."

"Didn't think he'd want to stick around after all the trouble swirlin' 'bout him like a Texas tornado. But she might have a better chance if you're the one makin' the swap, Barnett for her."

Slocum looked at Wilson, who scowled even more, then shook his head.

"Don't see how that's possible. He's a prisoner wanted for murder."

"How else you gonna get the lady back?" Herk asked.

"You butt out," Wilson said, his temper fraying visibly. Slocum knew the marshal was in waters too deep to swim.

"I kin act as go-between. Don't reckon Mr. Ralston'd trust either of you so much," Herk said. "Let me do some dickerin' and see what might be possible."

Slocum took the paper from the marshal and quickly scanned it.

"This doesn't say anything about where Ralston wants to make the swap. How'd you find him if you went?" Slocum stared at Herk and wondered at the crippled man's smugness. He looked full of himself, all prideful.

"There's only so many places he kin be," Herk said.

"Where?"

"Now, that's up to the marshal for me to say," Herk said.

"I don't want to get nobody else involved. This is serious enough business," Wilson said. "You tell us where we might find Ralston, and we'll take care of any palaverin'."

For a man who wanted to be in the middle of it all, Herk looked mighty pleased with this dismissal by the marshal. Slocum wondered what Herk's game was. He had made the offer to go to Ralston, but was pleased as punch when he was told he couldn't. How would he have acted if Wilson had given him the nod to talk to Ralston? Slocum almost took the marshal aside to make him change his mind.

"I kin unnerstand that, Marshal, I kin, I really kin. You and Slocum there, you go on out and rescue the little lady."

"Where's he most likely to be?" Slocum asked.

"If I was the one doin' the ridin' out—and the marshal jist said I wasn't—I'd go out to where the Little Scorpion Creek flows into the Clear Fork of the Brazos. That's right at the corner of Mr. Ralston's property, but he likes it best of all."

"How long you been in Abilene?" Slocum asked. Momentary fear crossed Herk's weathered face, then the smiling mask descended.

"Long enough to overhear how he's got a special cabin out there. He brags on it ever' chance he gits."

"That so, Marshal?"

Wilson shrugged and said, "Don't rightly know, but if Herk says it's so, it must be. Not many in these parts who know more 'n him."

"Though he's only passing through?"

"You want to git on the trail, Mr. Slocum, soon as you kin. It's a ride up there."

Again Slocum saw the veiled glee on Herk's face, but the advice was good.

"We taking Barnett?" Slocum asked.

"He stays in lockup, leastways 'til we find if Miz Holman's still alive."

For once, Slocum agreed with the lawman. It would be the height of foolhardiness to take Barnett out and find themselves in an ambush—or worse. Angelina might already be dead. His fingers curled into a fist, then relaxed as he became aware of Herk watching him as closely as he watched the gimpy man.

Slocum got his horse and mounted, slowly walking the gelding back and forth in front of the jail as Wilson worked inside. The lawman finally came out carrying his sawed-off shotgun.

"Had to leave word for a deputy on what to do with the prisoners," Wilson explained. "And I needed to make for certain sure I had the proper supplies." He held up a box of shotgun shells. The marshal was ready for a prolonged battle.

As Slocum and Wilson turned to leave, Herk waved to them and called, "Good luck, good luck!" Then the man turned and began talking to a pair of cowboys who had drifted over to see what the fuss was all about. Herk slapped one on the back, and they headed for the nearby saloon.

Something about the cowboy and Herk bothered Slocum, but he couldn't put his finger on it. When Wilson spoke, he ignored the pair and answered, "I doubt Ralston will have any of his hands with him."

"You sound mighty sure, Slocum."

"Because a man like Ralston would take care of his own problems."

"More like make his own danged problems," Wilson grumbled.

Slocum couldn't argue, but he had a good read on Ralston. The man was used to calling the shots. When Angelina hadn't given in right away and sold him the Circle H, he had taken it as a personal affront. He might have killed Michael Holman to buy the ranch because Holman had refused to give up what he saw as the beginning of a family property to hand down to his children.

Whenever he and Angelina had any.

Slocum knew the woman had lost more than her husband; she had lost her future to someone using a knife.

"You shouldn't be along, Slocum," the marshal said. He cast a sideways look, as if he didn't want to confront Slocum directly.

"I'm in this mud hole up to my hips," Slocum said. "You might need help with Ralston."

"He's one tough hombre, that I'll grant," Wilson said, "but I kin handle him. I done it before."

Slocum didn't say a word. He doubted that.

"Yup, I used to work fer him. 'Til the accident."

Slocum had heard about that and rode along in silence since the marshal seemed intent on supplying all the conversation, one-sided though it was.

"I made good money ridin' fer Monty Ralston. That's why I can't understand why he'd up and do a danged fool thing like kidnapping Miz Holman. Not to swap fer the likes of Barnett."

"What does he stand to gain?" Slocum said, thinking aloud. That bothered him. Did Ralston think all his troubles would go away if he sprang Barnett from jail this way? If

the Rangers were called in, his troubles would be starting.
Even if the sheriff came back from his assignation in the
next county, he might have more trouble on his fork than he
could swallow. Rich and powerful went a long way toward
doing what he pleased, but eventually the people got fed up
with things like murder and kidnapping a widow woman.

He rubbed his neck where Finch had tightened the noose.
Sometimes a crowd got out of control mighty fast.

"Monty Ralston is a complicated son of a buck. He thinks
all the time, always plannin' 'fore doin'."

To Slocum, that didn't sound like the hotheaded rancher
at all. He had never seen him when he wasn't about to burst
a blood vessel in his temple from getting too angry.

"Tell me about the Brazos and the Little Scorpion Creek.
Is there decent cover? Can he see us coming if we ride in
from the south, or should we circle and come at him from
a different direction? From opposite sides?"

"Yer askin' questions I don't rightly know. I heard about
the place, but I never been there."

Slocum thought on this real hard. The marshal of Abilene
had never ridden here, although it was on Ralston's property
and he had worked for the rancher, but a man who wasn't
able to do more than eavesdrop in saloons knew the locale.
Herk was a man of many parts, and Slocum wasn't sure he
liked any of them. Nothing got past the man, and he played
a deeper game than it appeared. He might cadge free drinks,
but the light in his eyes, brief though it was, when the marshal had told him to forget about riding along, had been
undeniable. Herk had wanted to remain behind, yet he knew
enough of the terrain where Ralston was to describe it
clearly.

"What do you know of him? Herk?"

"Why do you ask? I don't know much of anything. He
came into town a few weeks back, leastways I think he did.
I never saw him, and then he was everywhere, all the time
spyin' on everyone and askin' questions. Never too obvious,

but he found out where every skeleton was hidden. That's how he gets ever'one to buy him drinks."

"No matter what happens, he is there."

"I don't know what yer sayin', Slocum. Where else would he be?"

"I thought I saw him when Angelina tried to gun me down."

"She did that? When?"

Slocum ignored the question, pointing ahead.

"That the Brazos?"

"We kin water our mounts, then follow it to where the Little Scorpion flows into it."

"There's hardly enough for our horses," Slocum said, standing in the stirrups and eyeing the sluggishly flowing river. It might carry the name "river" but it was hardly more than a stream this time of year.

"Mine likes the taste o' mud. Comes from bein' brung up out here in West Texas."

"There's a dry streambed." Slocum's sharp eyes followed it as it meandered back into rolling hills. There were dozens of places where Ralston might ambush them, if he wanted.

"That's likely what we're huntin'," Wilson said. His voice took on a shakiness that betrayed his fear. He reached down and drew out his shotgun, broke it open, and inserted two shells. It closed with a metallic click that could be heard for a mile.

Slocum said nothing about that. If Ralston was on the lookout for them, there wasn't a great deal they could do to avoid being seen. He snapped the reins and started his horse walking up the middle of the dry creekbed. It might run full during spring rains, but now it was bone dry.

As he rode, Slocum kept a sharp eye out for the rancher.

"You think this is a wild-goose chase, Slocum?"

"Can't say. Herk was the one who decided this was the spot mentioned in the note Ralston sent. I couldn't make head nor tail out of it."

"I got the same feelin'. But what else kin we do?"

"Stop," Slocum said softly. "We can stop right here. See up ahead, in that stand of post oaks?"

"No, I—" Wilson bit off his words when Monty Ralston stepped out from behind a tree and brought a rifle to his shoulder.

"Where's Barnett? You were supposed to bring him."

"Where's Angelina Holman?" Slocum called back. "There's no trade until we know she's still alive."

"She's safe."

"No Barnett until we see her," Slocum called.

"Then we got a Mexican standoff," Ralston said. "I'm not telling where she is until I have Barnett beside me."

"Why'd you send the note to Herk?" Slocum asked.

"What's the difference, Slocum?" Wilson gestured for him to be quiet, but he did it by lifting the shotgun.

"Son of a bitch!" Ralston pulled the rifle stock into his shoulder and fired.

Wilson grunted as he dropped his shotgun. The weapon tumbled down and discharged when it hit the rocky riverbed. The twin barrels going off caused Slocum's horse to rear in fright. From the corner of his eye, he saw the marshal flailing on his own horse, then toppling off to land hard on the ground.

Ralston shot again as Slocum struggled to regain control of his horse. When he did, the rancher had disappeared into the wood area. Slocum drew his six-shooter, put his head down, and kicked at his horse, galloping forward. He reached the spot where Ralston had opened fire in time to see the man stepping up into the saddle on a horse only a dozen yards off.

Slocum fired. Ralston bent low and raced off. Slocum fired again, then lit out in pursuit. His horse was tired and slowly lost ground to Ralston's rested steed. He got off another shot, cursed, and emptied his six-gun at the fleeing man.

He kept riding, fumbling to reload. Attention on the cartridges going into his rechambered Colt Navy, he was taken by surprise when he looked up and saw a horse sprawled on the ground, feet kicking feebly. As he rode past, he saw that one of his bullets had struck the horse from behind and dug deep into the guts.

"Ralston? Where are you?" Slocum drew rein and looked around. The sound of a rifle cocking warned him.

He ducked low and fired across his body, more by instinct than skill. Slocum got his thumb on the hammer to cock the six-shooter again, but it wasn't needed. Sitting up in the saddle, he stared at the rancher's body on the ground. His lucky shot had drilled straight through Ralston's left eye, killing him instantly.

It was a lucky shot that saved his life—and unlucky for Angelina Holman. Ralston was the only one who knew where she was held captive, and he was very, very dead.

10

"Dead as a mackerel," Marshal Wilson said, shoving the toe of his boot into Ralston's unmoving side.

"You going to search him?"

Wilson looked at Slocum and scowled.

"Now why'd I go and do a thing like that? I ain't gonna rob him. I sure as hell ain't gonna split the contents of his pockets with the likes of you, even if I was so inclined."

"Angelina Holman," Slocum said, exasperated. "There might be some clue to where she is."

Wilson looked around, as if the woman might appear because Slocum named her. He pursed his lips, prodded Ralston again, and finally said, "He ain't gonna tell us, is he? Not dead, not from the way you shot him dead."

"He did his share of shooting at us," Slocum said, exasperation turning to anger. "I followed because you weren't able to."

"Nope, wasn't," Wilson said. "But you didn't have no call to kill him like this."

"It was self-defense."

"Says you, but then he ain't around to gainsay that, is he?"

For two cents Slocum would have emptied his Colt into the lawman. He dropped to his knees and began searching the dead rancher's pockets for anything that might tell him where Angelina was. He tossed everything he found out onto the ground so he could examine it bit by bit. Nothing gave him the slightest clue as to where Ralston held her. Slocum rocked back on his heels, feeling a desolation he had seldom experienced.

"He might have killed her," he told the marshal. "He could have buried her about anywhere on his ranch."

"Might not bother. Just leave her out for the coyotes. They're hungry varmints. Them and the buzzards. And bugs. Them bugs'll strip a corpse of its flesh in a week, sometimes less."

Slocum wondered if the marshal had a death wish egging him on this way, but the man seemed oblivious to the effect of his words. They had come here to rescue Angelina. The marshal had lost sight of that somehow.

"You taking him back to town, or are you leaving him for the coyotes and buzzards?"

"Leave him? Are you loco, Slocum? He's 'bout the biggest land owner in these parts. I got to take him back so's there's no trouble passing along his ranch to his next of kin."

"Who might that be?"

Wilson scratched his head, then said, "Cain't say. His wife upped and died a few years back. Had three sons and a daughter. All of them's dead, too, I've heard. He might have a will. I'll ask that shyster lawyer in town that took care o' his legal matters."

Slocum made one last survey of the debris he had taken from Ralston's pockets. A penknife, a few coins, a watch that ran twenty minutes slow—that was all. He hadn't expected him to have a map showing where he had hidden Angelina, or maybe he did. Swapping Barnett for the map would have been smart, and Wilson would have agreed to that. By coming along, Slocum had made sure such a trade would never have occurred. He had wanted to know Angelina was alive before making any deal.

But there wasn't a map. There wasn't a scrap of paper.

On impulse, Slocum grabbed Ralston's right hand and examined the fingers.

"What you lookin' for?"

"Ink. No trace of ink."

"Why'd there be ink?"

"From writing the notes, the one saying he had kidnapped Angelina and the one Herk brought from the courier."

"Maybe he washed his hands."

Slocum snorted at that. Ralston's hands were as filthy as his own.

"Might be he was a good writer, didn't spill the ink."

"Might be," Slocum said, not convinced. If he had to make a guess, someone else had written the notes for Ralston. But what that meant was beyond him, and it didn't alter the sad fact that Angelina was still missing.

"Help me git him o'er his horse. I'll ride him on back to Abilene," Wilson said. "You comin' with me?"

"I'll look for the woman," Slocum said.

"With the earth so dry and sunbaked, findin' a trail's gonna be nigh on impossible."

"Got to try."

"You might look for buzzards circlin' 'round up in the sky. That's usually the only way to find somebody out on the prairie."

Slocum considered how easy it would be to return to Abilene with two bodies slung over their horses. He could always say Ralston and Wilson shot it out and killed each other. But he wasn't a killer. Not like that. Wilson would have to do more than rile him with thoughtless words to merit a bullet in his gut followed by a painfully slow death.

"I'll find her," he said with more confidence than he felt.

"There's always that spot in the cemetery next to her husband." Wilson tugged on the reins of Ralston's horse and got the animal moving. He swung into his saddle and pain-fully settled himself, then rode away without so much as a glance back at Slocum.

He shot a black look at Wilson, then set to work. He might not be the best tracker in the West, but he was good. He returned to the spot where Ralston had first come out of the trees and backtracked to where the rancher had squatted down, smoking one cheroot after another. From the pile of ashes and stubs, he had been here a couple hours. Circling, then spiraling out, Slocum looked for tracks. He made sure he had the right ones left by Ralston, then carefully followed the crushed grass, broken twigs, scrapes, and patches of barely disturbed dust to get an idea of the direction Ralston had ridden coming to the oak grove.

It wasn't much, but it was all he had to go on. There wasn't any reason for Ralston to hide his trail since he'd anticipated Wilson giving in and turning over Barnett. In spite of himself as he rode, Slocum looked into the pure blue Texas sky for circling buzzards. He knew what that would mean, but he saw nothing to dash his hopes that Angelina still lived.

Somewhere.

In the oppressive heat, probably without water, she wouldn't live long. This added urgency to his search, but he was leery of riding too fast. He didn't want to lose the faint traces of Ralston's trail. The rancher had come straightaway from up along the dry creekbed, making Slocum think Angelina wasn't too far off.

By midafternoon he began to worry that he was wrong. A half-dozen miles lay behind him and where he had shot down Ralston, and he hadn't come across anything to give him any hope of finding Angelina, alive or dead.

The trail led to a stock pond. He had to push aside a dozen cattle to get his horse close enough to drink. He shoved his own head into the water and got some of the trail dust off his face and hands. Then he drank before pulling his gelding away. The sun was dropping low in the sky. Tracking after dark wasn't possible. He had seen some men who could do it using a lantern, but he wasn't that good, even if he had the lantern.

He looked around the stock pond. The cattle were bunching together and lowing as if something was wrong. Slocum went toward them, but they didn't move. Curious, he pushed through and stopped dead when the setting sun cast a shadow off a rusty hinge. Putting his shoulder down, he muscled the cattle away and kicked away some dust to expose a wood door mounted in a frame flush with the ground. Slocum's heart raced. He had followed Ralston this far. This might be what he sought.

He wanted to find Angelina when he pulled the stick from the hasp and cast it aside. The door creaked open on the rusty hinges and released a musty smell welling up from below. Coughing, he stuck his head down just below ground level and called out.

"Angelina? Are you here? Angelina?"

The whimpering sound was the most rewarding he had ever heard. Slocum swung around, got his feet into the hole, then dropped. He hit the ground sooner than he had expected, falling less than three feet in the darkness. He knelt and used the faint light filtering in over his shoulder to reach out. In a dark pit like this he might have touched a rattler or scorpion.

There was no mistaking Angelina's sleek leg.

"It's me, John," she said as she pulled away.

She was alive!

She continued to cry as he reached out, worked his way up her unseen leg, and finally got his hands around her waist so he could pull her toward him. At first she resisted, then she flowed into his arms. Awkwardly embracing, she cried until his shoulder was damp from her tears.

"I thought I would die here. I thought you'd never find me."

"Let's get out of this storm cellar."

He had seen such hidey-holes throughout Kansas but seldom in Texas. Ralston might have put it in as a place to take shelter from tornadoes or for some other reason. Whatever the original purpose, it had been turned into a cruel prison in the heat.

"I tried to get out. I banged on the door, tried to get it open, tried to push it out of the ground and escape, but I couldn't." Her filthy hands had broken nails where she had clawed at the hard-packed dirt in an attempt to tunnel past the door.

"It's all right now. Ralston is dead."

"No! He can't be!"

"What's wrong?" Slocum was startled by her vehement denial.

"I wanted to kill him with my own hands. I wanted him to suffer. That's all that kept me going!" She broke down crying again.

Slocum guided her around until she was directly under the opening, then boosted her to her feet. She almost collapsed. He stood and then climbed from the hole so he could pull her out.

She gasped and reached for him, using him to stand. Her weakness prevented her from walking without his help as she struggled to get to the stock pond.

"No water. He didn't give me any water."

"You can have all you want now," Slocum said, kicking a few balky cows from their way to the pond. Angelina dropped to her knees and kept her head underwater so long Slocum feared she was drowning. But before he could ease her back, she broke free, tossed her wet, black hair like a whip, and then returned so her face was only inches above the water. Cupping her hands, she scooped as much water as fast as she could into her mouth. Slocum went from worrying that she'd drown herself to fearing that she'd bloat like a thirsty horse.

Again she stopped just short of him stopping her.

She sat back on her heels, face lit by the last rays of the sun, tilted her head back, and simply smiled.

"I knew you would come," she whispered. "How, I didn't know, but you'd never let anything bad happen to me."

Slocum didn't bother telling her how lucky he had been to find her. If the cattle hadn't insisted on clumping around the door, he would have ridden on, never seeing where Ralston had locked her up.

He went and sat beside her, arms holding her. She settled down with only an occasional shudder.

"I'm not up to going back yet, John. I can't face them all."

"No need. We have water here, and I have supplies for a couple days." He went to kiss her, but she turned away. It wasn't the right time, and Slocum didn't press the issue.

"I've never been more afraid. I was scared when I realized Michael had been murdered, but this? The light poked in around the wood frame, but not enough to let me see. And it was so hot. My tongue felt like it swelled to a dozen times what it should have." She burrowed more into his arms. "Why do things like this happen?"

"There are men willing to do anything to get their way," he said. "Ralston won't bother you ever again."

"I hope he suffered when you shot him."

"I'll fix some supper. You up for that?"

"All right." She washed up some more, scrubbing to get the last traces of dirt from the storm cellar off her before agreeing to eat. Slocum had fixed the best he could, but Angelina picked at the food and finally told him she wanted to go to sleep.

He let her use his blanket while he paced around the stock pond, keeping the cattle away from her. He watched the stars pop out and then disappear under high, thin clouds that looked like gauzy curtains being drawn across the sky. Finally returning to where Angelina slept fitfully, he lay down with his head on his saddle and drifted off to sleep, the cold air his only blanket.

Slocum came awake with a start when the odor reached him. His hand had gone halfway to his six-shooter before he realized Angelina was up before him and fixing coffee.

She took a sip from his one tin cup, then held it out. "Here, have some," she said.

He took it and tried not to make a face. Her coffee was worse than his, and time and again he had used some of his brew to clean off tar. He drank, then handed it back to her for more. They finished breakfast in silence, then packed and got ready to return to Abilene.

"You want to go to town or your ranch?" he asked.

She hesitated, then said, "Town. I don't know what I want to do but being at the ranch isn't it. I might look for someone to buy the spread. Keeping it's not as important to me anymore, not after all this." She made a vague gesture with her hand, taking in the prairie and the storm cellar and the cattle. He knew what she meant.

"There's likely to be someone around willing to give the Circle H the attention it deserves."

"Our cattle never had Texas fever, no matter what they said. I heard the rumors, but they were wrong. We had some downers, but it wasn't the fever."

As they rode, Slocum in the saddle and Angelina behind him, arms circling his waist, they talked of inconsequential things. There wasn't time or call to do more.

It took them two days to return to Abilene. Slocum didn't want to exhaust his horse, and more important, he wanted to give Angelina the chance to get used to the idea of being surrounded by people again. She would have to tell the marshal all that had happened, and her ordeal would spread like wildfire through the cattle town, making her an overnight celebrity. Those who had worked for Ralston and those who were beholden to him—Slocum wondered about Wilson— would call her a liar and worse, but there would be those who believed. That would be good enough to help her through the tough times until she could sell her ranch.

"There it is," Slocum said in the late afternoon of the second day on the trail. "In all its glory."

"Abilene," she said, making it sound like a curse word. "Let's get it over with."

"Straight to Marshal Wilson?"

She pressed her cheek against his back. He wasn't sure if she was crying again. A snap of the reins got the horse moving slowly toward the main street, but Slocum came to a complete halt at the edge of town.

"What's wrong, John?"

"Don't know for sure, but it looks like some kind of celebration."

"It's weeks until the Fourth of July."

He didn't have the feeling in his gut that what was gripping Abilene was that kind of celebration. There was a more frantic feel to this, one of desperation.

One like he had seen too often at public hangings.

"Maybe you should go on out to your ranch after all," he said.

"No, let's go. To the marshal. I want to get this over, telling him what happened. Otherwise, I might lose my nerve."

The crowd became more boisterous the closer to the middle of town they rode. From horseback he saw the gallows and the hanged man slowly swinging in the arid wind.

He started to veer away so Angelina wouldn't see, but she had.

"Who?"

"I don't know," he said but that was a lie. He knew. Barnett had been strung up. He had been executed for killing Michael Holman—and Slocum didn't believe he was the murderer.

11

"Why are they celebrating?" Angelina asked in a choked voice. "They just hung a man. You know who it is. Tell me." She strained to look around Slocum from her vantage behind him.

"It's Barnett." Turning to look over his shoulder, he watched her reaction. Shock was replaced with disbelief and then a glow of vengeance came to her eyes, turning them into bright beacons.

"He killed Michael. He deserved it."

"Are you going to join the cheering?" Slocum looked out over the crowd. Barnett had been swung only a few minutes earlier from the crowd's reaction. They were building up to a real celebration.

"Why not?" Angelina turned angry now. "He was a killer!"

"Don't dispute that," Slocum said. Barnett had likely killed more than his share of men in his day, but Slocum wasn't in any mood to argue with her, especially since he had nothing to prove that someone other than Barnett had killed her husband. For all he knew as a fact, Ralston had ordered his foreman to stab his rival—and Barnett had. But the way Barnett had reacted in the jail when shown the knife used to kill Holman bothered Slocum. It wasn't the look of a man responsible for the death.

Barnett might have gloated or he might have bragged on how Holman had died. He had denied it, knowing Ralston would try to get him free no matter what he said. And Slocum doubted Ralston had killed Holman either. From what he had heard, and Angelina even admitted it, their spread was too small for Ralston to worry over. Eventually he would have gobbled up the Circle H. All it would take was another long drought.

Even if Ralston had wanted to speed up matters, killing Holman and leaving his body where it could be found was stupid, and whatever else Slocum thought of Ralston, stupid wasn't in the mix. Even if he had flown off the handle and killed Holman in a sudden violent rage, he would have cooled down soon enough to take the body and dump it out on the prairie, where it wasn't likely to ever be found.

The storm cellar he had used as a prison for Angelina would have made a fine grave. And there had to be other places on his ranch that would successfully hide the result of a momentary murderous impulse. Mostly, though, Slocum knew men as rich and powerful as Ralston could thumb their nose at the law. He could have always told Marshal Wilson that he had killed in self-defense. Until Ralston had shoved the lawman in public and humiliated him, Wilson had gone out of his way to defend the rancher.

With Angelina going on about Barnett's guilt and her speculation on his eternal damnation, he turned his horse toward the jail. He wanted to talk to Wilson and find what had happened to hasten the execution.

"Why don't you get yourself a room, get cleaned up, and rest a spell?" Slocum suggested as they passed the hotel. "I'll be back and we can get something to eat."

"Very well." Angelina had turned icy toward him since

he failed to share her enthusiasm for Barnett's necktie party. She dropped, then hesitated, looking up at him. "How will I pay for it?"

"Take this," Slocum said, fumbling in his pocket and handing her a silver cartwheel. "I'll pay the rest when I get back."

She silently took the silver dollar and went into the hotel. Slocum watched her. Even as filthy as she was, as disheveled from her ordeal and the ride back to Abilene, she was a fine-looking woman. His attention was pulled away when he caught something moving fast just at the corner of his vision. He saw a man hidden in shadow running down an alley next to the hotel. Slocum called out, but the man turned the corner and disappeared without breaking stride. Slocum shook his head at being so jumpy, then rode slowly to the jail to find Wilson.

The marshal was outside talking to a small crowd, waxing eloquent—or as eloquent as he could get—over the execution.

"Be sure you git that there quote right," Wilson said, peering over the top of a notebook held in the hands of an earnest young man whom Slocum took as a reporter.

The young man scribbled and finally read back what he had written. Wilson beamed.

"That's it. You got me jist right on the matter."

Slocum dismounted and waited for the interview to end. The reporter rushed away after assuring the marshal it would be in the morning edition.

"Why'd you let him swing?" Slocum asked without preamble.

"Good to see you again, too, Slocum. You find her?"

"I did. Ralston had her locked up in a storm cellar."

"At his ranch house?" Wilson's eyes went wid. "You poked around the Ralston house and found her there?"

"She was at a stock pond. I reckon Ralston used the storm cellar there for storage as well as shelter from tornadoes, but there wasn't anything but Angelina in it when I got there."

"Least Ralston didn't kill her."

Slocum studied the marshal, wondering if he was making a roundabout accusation about the way he had cut down Ralston. He couldn't tell. The rancher's death had changed Wilson, given him confidence and made him seem more arrogant.

"Why'd you let them string up Barnett? He didn't kill Holman."

"It was his knife."

"The knife was found in his gear, but he denied that it was his."

"What's a killer likely to do? Brag on the murder?"

Slocum had his own opinion on that. Barnett likely would have, if he had killed Holman. He wasn't so self-possessed that he'd take credit for another man's kill. Slocum corrected himself. Barnett hadn't been.

"Did he get a trial?"

"I didn't think there was no need," Wilson said. "A waste of taxpayer money gettin' a judge into town, hirin' a jury, and rilin' ever'one up. I jist cut to what was gonna happen anyway."

"Didn't take long to build the gallows," Slocum said.

"Got a good deal from two carpenters."

"I'm sure you saved the town a lot of money."

Wilson looked hard at Slocum and asked, "Are you ridiculin' me, Slocum?"

"Wouldn't think of it, Marshal. Wouldn't think of it." With that Slocum scooped up his horse's reins and walked away. Barnett had been railroaded for the crime, and Slocum had the feeling there was something more to the hanging. Wilson had grown a pair since returning and didn't have any trouble going ahead with the hanging on his own.

Slocum knew he could dig into the matter and find the real reason Barnett was hanged so quickly, but getting out of Abilene appealed more to him by the minute. He'd see what he could do to help Angelina sell her ranch, then he would ride on. He had tried to go west before. North appealed more to him now, maybe Kansas or Nebraska.

Anywhere but Texas.

He stabled his horse and returned to the hotel, to find a long line of men stretching from the lobby. Angry arguments raged inside. Slocum started to push past a man in the doorway, only to be shoved back.

"You wait your turn!"

"Turn?" Slocum didn't like the way the man had jostled him. "What's going on?"

"Town's got a brand-new whore, and she's mighty fine. Only charges a dime to touch her titties. Two bits gets you into bed with her."

Slocum started to push past the man again, and again he was shoved away.

"I said you gotta wait yer turn. Sloppy seconds ain't good enough for you?"

"Seconds?" The man in line behind laughed. "Can't count high enough. Heard she wants to have every man in town 'fore sundown."

"She'd better hurry," piped up another.

"With you, that's not a concern," yet another man called. This set off a minor scuffle.

"Let me inside," Slocum said to the man blocking his way.

"You wait your turn."

"I'm not in line for any whore."

The man laughed harshly. Then he poked Slocum in the chest with his fingertips.

"Says you. We saw you payin' her 'fore you rode away. You mighta paid her already but you have to wait."

"Angelina?" The name slipped from his lips unbidden.

"That's her name."

The leer on the man's lips was too much for Slocum. He didn't even wind up for the punch he drove into the mouth.

He felt teeth yield and lips crush, then sticky blood ooze out. The man staggered away, holding his mouth and trying to cry out. His tongue might have gotten bit from the noises. Slocum didn't much care. He shoved the man hard to get him out of the way and went into the lobby, where the clerk argued with the men at the foot of the stairs.

"You can't—"

"I can," Slocum said. His bloody fist and grim expression got him past the clerk and onto the stairs. His tread was so heavy, boards sagged under his weight. He reached the landing and looked back. The crowd was getting nastier, and the clerk wasn't likely to hold them back much longer.

Without any idea which room Angelina had checked into, he knocked sharply on each door in turn until he got a frightened "go away" that sounded like her. He rattled the doorknob. Locked.

"It's Slocum. Let me in."

"John?"

The key turned and a single bloodshot blue eye peered out. She had been crying some more. He pushed in, not giving her a chance to open the door farther.

"What the hell's going on?"

"I . . . I don't know. I checked in and then a cowboy came to the door. I thought it was you. He held up a wad of greenbacks and said lewd things. I got him out, but there were a couple more behind him. Then there were dozens!"

"They're lined up out in the street, all thinking you're a whore and open for business."

"I never—"

"No, you didn't," he said. She came into his arms. He held her until she stopped quaking. "Somebody passed the word and caused this mess."

He remembered seeing the man running down the alley and wondered if that wasn't the cause of the rumor. The man had seen Slocum give Angelina a dollar for the room and overheard his promise to be back with more, if she needed it.

That was thin, but it was all he could think of.

"What are we going to do, John? I . . . can't stay here now."

He poked his head out the door and saw the clerk had either been overwhelmed or had given up trying to hold back the horny cowboys.

The thud of boots on the stairs warned him of the folly of opening the door again.

"Out the window."

"But I can't do that!"

He caught her around the waist, lifted her legs, and spun her so her feet went through the open window. Angelina scrambled, trying to find purchase on the sloping eaves at the side of the hotel. Slocum held her for a moment, then let her go as the door burst inward. Spinning, he whipped out his six-shooter and fired three times, the bullets going to the side to break a mirror, above to shatter the transom, and finally into the door itself to send a cascade of splinters into the hall beyond. The lead cowboy yelped, ducked, fell on the shattered mirror, and added to the confusion with loud cries of pain. The man behind tried to run and crashed into two others in the hall. The pandemonium was all Slocum could have asked for.

Holstering his six-gun, he stepped through the window, then jumped, hitting the ground near Angelina. He grabbed her hand and pulled the dazed woman behind him like a child's toy. Ducking down the alley where he had seen the fleeing man earlier, he followed the same route and came out in the main street between two saloons. Two Cyprians stood on the boardwalk, passing a cigarette back and forth. They hardly took notice of Slocum and Angelina, but from inside that saloon came angry cries.

What wasn't being delivered at the hotel was in demand here. The two women finished their smoke and went back into the saloon to boisterous customers whose appetites had been churned by Angelina's denied beauty.

"I want to go home, John. I want to go home."

"Your ranch?"

She nodded, her hair in wild, dark disarray. He pushed some of it from her eyes, then tugged to get her moving to the stables. Once there, Slocum looked around for the stableman but didn't see him. Considering the man's predilection for drink, he was likely at a nearby saloon. Or he might have heard about the new talent in town and had lined up with the other men at the hotel.

"Take that one," Slocum said, pointing to a small mare. "Use this saddle and blanket." He heaved the equipment from a box. The stableman had done some work. The saddle was freshly cleaned and soaped.

"We can't steal a horse."

"I'm paying for it," Slocum said, fishing in his pocket. All he had was eighteen dollars in folding money. He shoved it onto a nail in the stall where Angelina struggled to get the mare saddled. It was hardly enough, but Slocum thought Abilene owed Angelina something for all she had been through. The stableman would only pour the money down his gullet. To Slocum's way of thinking, everyone was coming out ahead on the deal.

Angelina had a horse, and the livery owner had something to show for it. He could take the eighteen dollars to a bar and drink it up, complaining about how thieves had stolen the best horse he had.

Slocum smiled wryly. The stable owner might even cadge a few free drinks if he spun a good enough tale of thievery and woe.

He led his horse from the stables, Angelina close behind. Once outside, they stepped up and turned away from the crowd still yelling and causing a ruckus at the hotel. As they rode from Abilene, Slocum saw a familiar figure sitting on a rain barrel, swinging his good leg back and forth.

Herk waved to them. Slocum didn't bother waving back.

"Who was that?"

"Nobody important," Slocum said. "Head off the road. That way, across the prairie."

"If we follow the road . . ."

"They'll think that's what we did. This way we get to your ranch sooner and let them follow the bends in the road."

"Who're you talking about?"

Slocum didn't rightly know. He doubted any of the frustrated men would pursue them. Instead, they'd take their business to other soiled doves or drink away the money they had been so eager to press onto Angelina. Whatever happened, the woman was well rid of them and Abilene.

After a few minutes of galloping, he slowed the pace and saw that she was openly crying. Tears left muddy tracks on her cheeks. She didn't even bother wiping them away. Sobs wracked her body as she was bounced around on the horse. The mare's gait was off and would make for a tired rider by the end of the day.

"What did I do to deserve this?" Angelina caught her breath and held back her tears now. "I never did anything so bad that would mean Michael's death or being kidnapped or . . . or that!" She half turned and looked back in the direction of Abilene. Slocum knew what she meant by "that."

He often wondered why a storm cloud followed some people and rained on them constantly. Angelina had been favored with good looks and a quick mind, but every other portion of her life was lower than a snake's belly.

"What's the next town over?" Slocum asked.

"What? The one where . . . where I tried to shoot you?" She wiped her nose on her sleeve and sniffed. "That's Hedison. Why?"

"Might be a good place to go, after you've had a chance to get what you need from your house. It's close enough for you find a banker willing to buy your ranch but far enough away from Abilene so nobody from there will trouble you."

"A banker? Oh, I see. Let the bank handle the sale. Why not?" She sniffed again and looked at him. He had seen forlorn women before but seldom this distraught. "I'm not thinking right, John. Don't leave . . . until . . . until things are more settled. Please."

Slocum realized what he was getting himself in for when he said, "Yes."

She swallowed hard but stopped crying. They rode in silence, Slocum letting her take the lead since he knew only the general direction of her ranch. It was well past sundown when they found the weed-overgrown road, and Angelina turned down it.

She drew rein just inside a low fence intended to keep the chickens from getting out. From the lack of poultry and abundance of feathers, she and her husband had been gone long enough for coyotes and foxes to dine on the chickens.

"Not much, is it?"

"It's plenty since it's yours," he answered.

She heaved a deep sigh and urged her mare forward, stopping at the side of the house. Slocum considered simply leaving her and riding on, but he had promised to see her through the next few days after she settled in Hedison.

"I'll see to the horses," he said, catching the mare's reins and riding toward the barn.

The door leading in needed repair but not as much as many of the places he had seen on the prairie. It was difficult for only a man and a woman to keep up a spread without hands or a large family to pitch in with the chores. He put the horses in clean stalls and did what he could, finding very little in the way of hay or grain to feed them. He went to the pump out back and made certain the horses had plenty of water after the long ride from town.

Only then did he go to the house, not sure what to do. He could sleep in the barn. That would suit him just fine, but Angelina had seemed to need comforting. What more he could do was a mite hazy. He went up the steps into the kitchen, where she worked on fixing a meal for them.

"Set yourself down. It won't be much but it's got to be

better than the moldy jerky and hard bread you've been eating."

Slocum gingerly sat in a chair, as if any sound might disturb the picture of domestic tranquility. Angelina knew her way around the kitchen and whipped up a decent plate of food. Slocum ate with real appetite but noticed she only sat across from him and watched with hollow, empty eyes.

"We can leave first thing in the morning," he said.

"All right. There's not much I want to pack. Some clothing. A few pieces of jewelry my mama gave me."

"You don't have any family? At all?"

"I'm like you now, John. A drifter," she said. She smiled but no humor came to her eyes. "All my people are gone."

With that she got to her feet and went into the small bedroom, where Slocum saw her throwing things into a traveling case. She hesitated when she held a picture frame, as if deciding what to do with it. She added it to the contents. Eventually she ran out of space and stopped, returning to take his empty plate.

"You had a good appetite."

"Good food."

"I'm packed. All I need." She stood a little straighter. "All I want to take. The rest can be sold with the spread."

She dropped the plate into a bucket and turned toward him; their eyes locked. Angelina reached up and began unbuttoning her blouse, her intent obvious.

A rock smashed the window behind her, causing her to cry out in fright and jerk to one side in time to avoid being hit with a flaming torch. In seconds the kitchen was engulfed in fire.

12

Angelina stood frozen as flames rushed up all around her. Slocum kicked over the table, grabbed the legs, and heaved, throwing the table past the woman and out the window. For a moment, the yawning hole was blocked and the fire flickered. He followed the table and grabbed her, spinning her around and bodily flinging her into the bedroom. Then Slocum slapped out the tiny fires that tried to gain a foothold in his clothing.

Holes smoldering where the sparks had ignited, he stumbled into the bedroom and looked for a door.

"There isn't one," Angelina called from the other side of the bed.

"Out the window. Wait, stop!" He thought only of escaping the fire that spread rapidly through the kitchen and now licked at the ceiling. In minutes—less!—the house would be nothing but charred, smoking remains. But he had forgotten whoever had flung the torch through the window.

Angelina used her case to knock out the window and started through when loud shouts from outside told Slocum his worry had been confirmed. An instant after the outcry came a hail of bullets. Again he tackled the woman and carried her to the floor as a hail of lead ripped through the air above them.

"What are we going to do?"

"Get out of here somehow," he said, choking on the smoke. Near the floor he found it easier to breathe, but only inches higher, toward the window, he had to hold his breath or pass out from the suffocating smoke.

Worse, the gunfire through the window started up again anytime he showed himself.

"Who is it? Who's doing this?" Angelina broke out crying again and sat, back against the wall and hugging herself.

"Let's find out," Slocum said. He drew his six-shooter, took Angelina's hand, and yanked her to her feet. She grabbed her case and clutched it to her chest. More lead came their way, but Slocum returned fire. He saw where the muzzle flashes blazed in the darkness and aimed just above them. He was sure he winged at least two of the gunmen.

He shoved her out the window; Angelina tumbled over the wall and flipped around to land flat on her back, still holding her case. This saved her life again as part of the roof came crashing down in a shower of sparks. She shrieked and thrust the case upward reflexively. The debris slid to one side, leaving her unharmed. Slocum hurriedly came through the window and knelt beside her, firing at any muzzle flash he saw until his Colt Navy came up empty.

By now Angelina had regained her feet and led the way. Slocum wasn't sure where she ran but had no choice but to follow. She started to go down into a root cellar, but he stopped her.

"We'll be trapped there."

"No, we won't. Please, John, I know what I'm doing."

Heavy gunfire forced Slocum to follow her into the storm cellar. The bullets dug holes in the heavy wood and then the closed door muffled the gunshots. Slocum clung to the rope on the door to hold it shut in the complete darkness.

"What do we do now?" he asked. Slocum looked away when the sudden flare of a lantern blinded him. Squinting, he saw her holding up the lantern.

"This way." She paused, then said, "Can you bring my valise?"

Slocum was torn between taking the time to reload and doing as she asked since she worked hard at the far wall.

He picked up the bullet-ridden case as Angelina pried open a wood panel to reveal a low-ceilinged tunnel leading away. Slocum wasted no time following, then pulled the planks behind him to close up the passage.

"The light!" His warning alerted her to shield the light with her body.

The storm cellar echoed with repeated shots, then shouts as men dropped into the hole. Slocum pressed his eye to a knothole and caught sight of one man.

"Finch," he said when he recognized the cowboy. He lifted his pistol and would have tried firing through the peephole but remembered in time his pistol was empty. Such an abortive attack would only draw unwanted attention. He heard Angelina moving behind him but dared not move, not yet.

"Where'd they go?"

"You just thought you seen 'em come here. There's so damn much smoke from the house, they musta run off into the night."

"Naw, they died in the fire. You were both seeing ghosts."

The argument raged for almost a minute, causing Slocum to get antsy. He was usually a patient fighter, but now he wanted to attack. Only the knowledge that Angelina would also die kept him frozen in place.

"Might be another way out," Finch said. He moved around, using his pistol butt to rap on the wood walls. Slocum held his breath as Finch moved closer. When he got to this panel, he'd hear nothing but a hollow ring and know where his victims had fled.

He stopped just inches away when another man stuck his head down and called out, "We gotta go. The weeds are catchin' fire. We're gonna burn if we stay."

"Just a minute more."

"Now," insisted the cowboy, who disappeared.

Finch grumbled but immediately left the root cellar.

"Can we go now?" Angelina asked in a low voice.

Slocum made sure the panel would stay in place if he released it, then turned and pushed her along the tunnel. She hurried, half bent over because of the low ceiling. Slocum's back ached by the time she stopped and pointed up to a trapdoor.

"It opens in the barn," she said. "Michael dug the tunnel so he could get to the barn and tend the animals in case of a tornado."

"That was right thoughty of him," Slocum said dryly. He motioned for her to extinguish the lantern, then pushed up the trap and peered around. It took him a few seconds until his eyes adapted to the dark. Flickering light from the direction of the house caused the horses to kick at their stalls and whinny in growing fear.

Like a snake, he slithered through the small space between the ground and the lifted trapdoor. After duck-walking to the barn door and looking out, he relaxed. Finch and his men had mounted and ridden off. The glow from the burning house afforded him enough light to reload his six-shooter, then slip back into the barn, where Angelina was already saddling the horses.

"The cowboys have lit out," he told her. She turned and stared at him, her face bleak. The light from the fire danced in her eyes.

"You recognized them, didn't you?"

"One was Finch, the man who might have gunned down Macauley back in Abilene," he said.

"I know him. He's top hand at the T Bar T. He works for George Lawrence."

Slocum made sure he repeated this over and over so it was etched into his memory. He owed Finch for the necktie party and now this despicable crime. Not only had Finch and his boys wanted to burn out Angelina, they wanted to kill her.

"What does Finch have against you? Or is it his boss?"

"Michael and Mr. Lawrence got along all right," she said, keeping a tight grip on the skittish horse as she led it from the barn.

She and Slocum turned their horses' faces from the dancing flames, mounted, and rode straight off into the night. He hoped they were heading in the same direction taken by Finch. A quick touch on the ebony butt of his six-shooter assured him how that encounter would turn out. He wasn't about to give Finch a third try at killing him.

"Which way are we riding?" Angelina asked after they'd ridden more than a half hour away from her house. She looked up but clouds obscured the stars.

Slocum worked his way through the entire sky, hunting for pieces of constellations he recognized. He finally found the Scorpion in the southern sky and told her.

"Hedison is to the southwest of our—my—house," she said. Angelina fell silent as she took in the idea that even this was denied her now. She had lost the property when her husband had been murdered, and now the house with all her belongings was gone, too.

Slocum saw that she had lashed her valise to the mare's rump. That was her entire heritage, whatever she had packed before Finch set fire to her house.

"How far?"

"Close to twenty miles. There's no way I can make it tonight, and my horse is starting to falter."

"Might step in a prairie dog hole in the dark, too," Slocum said. He wished he knew where Finch had gone. He asked Angelina where the T Bar T lay.

"It's northeast of us. It's not half the size of Ralston's spread, but it's easily twice the size of the Circle H."

Slocum listened with half an ear. He strained to hear the night sounds. He caught the distant howl of a coyote, but nearer came small animals running about. Insects buzzed and other noises assured him that Finch was already long gone and not waiting in ambush somewhere near.

There was no good reason for the cowboy to believe they would come this way when he wasn't sure what had happened to them. As they rode, Slocum relaxed even more. He kept a sharp eye on the sky and saw more bits of constellations to guide them.

"There's the Big Dipper," he said, pointing to the north. "The sky's clearing to the north."

"But not to the south," Angelina said. "That's where storms come from this time of year. The wind blows the rain off the Gulf of Mexico."

Slocum took a deep whiff of the night air and nodded. He smelled rain in the air. Being caught in the open during a frog strangler of a Texas storm wasn't to his liking.

"Anywhere nearby we can take shelter?"

"There's an old cabin somewhere around here," she said. "It's got a windmill tower by it. The windmill doesn't work—Michael took the blades down to use for our own windmill, but he never got the pump working right."

Slocum saw a starlit trail cut by hundreds of hooves over the past few months and followed it. Angelina had gone from crying to talking incessantly about what she and Michael had planned and how it would never happen now.

"There," he said, pointing to a dark shape rising from the prairie. "A windmill tower."

"Just in time," she said. "I just got hit in the face with a raindrop. A big one, too. We're in for a hard shower."

They'd barely reached the ramshackle cabin by the time the storm hit. Angelina protested when Slocum led their horses into the small cabin, but he wanted them out of the rain, too.

"I don't want to get stepped on in my sleep," she said querulously. "Can't we leave them outside?"

"In this rain?" Sheets of water cascaded from the sky, making it impossible to see more than a few feet. With the starlight blotted out, Slocum thought they had been swallowed by some looming, dark, dank beast.

"They're animals."

"They're what we need to get us to Hedison," he reminded her.

Angelina grumbled, got her blanket, and curled up in the far corner of the single-room cabin, her back to him. Slocum looked out, didn't see anything or anyone moving in the rain, and finally sank down, back against a wall in an effort to find as dry a spot as possible. He was soaked through and through by dawn, but at least he had gotten some much-needed sleep, even if nightmares of fleeting figures and ambushes and lynchings filled his dreams.

In the morning they were both quiet, lost in their own thoughts. As if they finally locked into the other's mind, they looked up at the same time and spoke.

"You first, John," she said. "What is it?"

"Ride on into Hedison alone," he said. "I want to scout for the cowboys that burned you out."

"To make sure they're not following us?"

"They can't know," he said, "that we escaped the fire. This makes it easier for me to do something about them."

"You're not talking about turning them over to the marshal, are you?" She shivered. Just a little. Her blue eyes appeared dull now, their luster gone because of all she had endured.

"There's no evidence against them," Slocum said. "One would alibi for the other."

"You might go to the T Bar T and tell Mr. Lawrence what his men have done."

"That's not going to work if Lawrence told them to do it. You said that the land was more valuable to him than it would have been to Ralston. Might be, Lawrence is behind everything."

"Including Michael's death?" She shook her head. "Barnett had the knife."

"He was a dupe. Somebody planted the knife in his gear when they found out the doctor kept the knife tip buried in your husband."

Slocum saw tears welling in Angelina's eyes and knew he had been too straightforward, but he wasn't the kind to put a spoonful of sugar on anything like death. It ought to be cruel and terrible to remind everyone how fragile life was and to hang on as hard as you could. Make dying too easy and people got careless.

"Let them go," she said. "I need to get over Michael's death, and seeing Finch and the others strung up or shot down isn't going to bring him back. It won't bring back my house and everything in it. That . . . that was the last thread I had holding me to him. All we'd done together, it's all lost now."

"You have your memories," Slocum said. "Those are more powerful than any chair or table or picture."

"I suppose you're right. It just doesn't seem like that now." She looked at him hard and the tears began to flow. She let them dribble down her cheeks before looking away. "Let's hurry, John. The sooner I'm in Hedison, the sooner I can see the ranch sold and you can be on your way."

He said nothing to her as he packed up their gear, saddled, and the two of them rode in silence.

13

"You going to stay here or move on?" Slocum asked. It was the first time he had spoken in more than an hour. There didn't seem to be much else to say to Angelina. She certainly had nothing to say to him—nothing that would have convinced him to stay with her.

Slocum thought she was a beautiful woman, but she wasn't thinking straight this soon after her husband's death and getting burned out by Finch and his men. Too much had been heaped on her. She needed time to sort through it all and decide what her life ought to be like. In a month or a year. Slocum knew there wasn't any set number of days for the shock and sadness to fade away. He still felt some sorrow at his brother's death and the way his parents had died before he could get back to Slocum's Stand in Calhoun, Georgia, after the war.

He felt the sadness, but it didn't make him wake in the night, sobbing, the way Angelina's sorrow did her. If they had met earlier or maybe if their trails crossed again in a year, things would be different. Slocum didn't want to play savior to anyone, even a woman as lovely as Angelina Holman.

She looked down from the low hill at Hedison. Her expression was neutral, but her shoulders were tense, giving him the answer. She was still too near her ranch and all that had happened there to be comfortable here.

"Might," she said at length. "Is there a lawyer in town to handle the sale? Michael never cottoned much to bankers. Didn't have anything to say one way or the other about lawyers."

"Lawyers are like cockroaches. They're everywhere. You shine some light under a basket and hint that there's money to be had selling a ranch and they'll line up from here to Abilene."

"One lawyer will do me."

"There's got to be one," he assured her.

They rode down the hillside and to the road splitting Hedison in half. There were a few streets parallel to the main one but damned few. Abilene was a cattle town and catered to the hordes of cowboys off the surrounding ranches. Hedison survived from a few ranches but probably more from farmers. This would be a quieter town, one without the gunfire and sudden death offered by Abilene.

As they rode, Slocum felt the eyes of the townspeople on them. He doubted they were staring at him as much as they were at Angelina and wondering what brought her there. Slocum was obviously a drifter, but she looked the part of a ranch wife.

"Howdy, folks," said a small, wiry man who stepped out into the street in front of them. The badge on his vest told the story. "Welcome to Hedison."

"Marshal," Slocum greeted. "Just the man we wanted to find."

"Now how's that?" The lawman turned slightly, as if preparing to throw down on Slocum. "You got reason to seek me out?"

"Not you personally. Just the town marshal. This is Mrs.

Holman, and her husband died recently. She wants to sell the Circle H ranch and needs somebody to represent her legally."

"We got a couple lawyers. Neither's worth the gunpowder to blow 'em to hell. Don't take offense at such blue language, ma'am," the marshal said. His attitude toward her changed subtly when Slocum had declared her to be a grieving widow. In every small town it was the same. If you were a loose cannon, you were suspect. If you could be placed in a box, neatly labeled, and placed on the shelf in an appropriate spot, everything was just fine.

"Which is the best of the sorry lot, Marshal?" Angelina asked.

"That'd be Lee Dawson, and I'm not sayin' that just 'cuz he's my sister's oldest. He hasn't screwed up as many cases as Tom Underwood. He's not as much of a drunk either. Not so far, though Lee has been known to tipple a bit too much on Saturday night over at the saloon."

"You make them both sound so appealing," Angelina said, smiling.

"Just tellin' it like it is. Circle H?" The marshal scratched the back of his neck. "That's closer to Abilene than here, ain't it?"

"Mrs. Holman found too many memories in Abilene and wanted to make a clean break."

"How's that?"

"Her husband is buried there. Everything in town reminds her of better days," Slocum said. He saw Angelina turned glum as he furnished the reasons the marshal might believe and knew he was hitting the bull's-eye one after the other. He made no mention of Finch and how the T Bar T boys had burned her out.

"You'll want to find a place to stay?" The marshal looked hard at Slocum.

"I can sleep in the livery stable, but Mrs. Holman would be better served at a hotel or boardinghouse."

"Elena Gomez runs a nice place on the far side of town. Heard tell she has a room for let."

"Much obliged, Marshal."

"Marshal Hooker. No relation to the damned Federal general."

"Glad to hear it," Slocum said, getting a smile from the lawman. The smoother things went now, the quicker he could be on his way out of town. San Antonio beckoned. Or perhaps El Paso. He had been on his way there when he stopped over in Abilene. Adobe Walls lay to the north, but it would take a powerful lot of riding before he found another town, and for some reason he found himself wanting people around. Not many, but some.

Slocum introduced himself, and the marshal said, "I'll see the lady on down the road to Señora Gomez's house. Stable's yonder, Slocum." The marshal pointed. Slocum saw an anvil out front and knew the black smithy was likely in the same barn.

"Come by later, Jo—Mr. Slocum," Angelina said. "Perhaps Señora Gomez will be able to set another place at the dinner table."

Slocum looked up and guessed the time was just past noon. Staying for dinner meant spending a night in Hedison when he could put five miles or more behind him before sundown.

"Sounds good."

"She's a mighty fine cook. You can tell that by Señor Gomez's waist size." Hooker arched back and patted the air a couple feet in front of his own lean, flat belly.

"After eating trail grub, that is mighty enticing," Slocum said. He tipped his hat as Angelina rode on. He heaved a sigh and walked his horse to a saloon. There was a second one halfway down the street, but Hedison didn't sport them side by side for a hundred yards along both sides of the main thoroughfare like Abilene. That told him as much about the town as anything. Peaceful. Angelina could do worse than settling here, finding herself a trade and a decent man. A merchant, maybe, could probably give her the kind of quiet life she deserved without gunplay and instant death.

As Slocum stepped up to the swinging doors leading into the saloon, he paused. From the corner of his eye he caught a shadow, moving fast. He spun, hand going to his six-shooter, but nothing was there. He squeezed his eyes shut hard, then opened them slowly. This wasn't the first time he had seen the specter, and it was beginning to annoy him. The times he had been out in the desert without enough water and hallucinating hadn't been this unsettling. He knew he wasn't seeing a mirage now, though. Something was there and always just beyond his ability to focus on it.

It was as if someone quick on his feet wanted to stay hidden from him.

Slocum walked to the side of the saloon and looked around. There might have been footprints in the dust, but it was so dry he couldn't tell. The scuffs ran toward the rear of the saloon. On impulse, Slocum went and looked around there. A man slept under an empty wagon. Otherwise, there wasn't anybody in sight. From the snoring, the man had been taking his siesta for quite a while, and Slocum wasn't going to wake him to find out what he already knew.

The man had seen nothing.

He returned to the front of the saloon and paused again. A curious tension in the air made him slip his six-gun halfway from the holster to reassure himself it could get into his hand fast, if needed.

The street was almost empty. A wagon rattled along to the general store, a farmer looking for supplies from the way the driver was dressed. Two men played mumblety-peg, the thunk of their knife momentarily louder than anything else in Hedison. The sound was quickly smothered when a man and a woman began arguing in front of the bakery.

An ordinary day in Hedison. Slocum spun rapidly, thinking to catch sight of the ghostly shadow, but he saw nothing.

He went into the saloon and ordered a beer. Two others were drinking, one whiskey and the other warm beer like he did. Slocum was less interested in whiskey to kill the pain of riding for days than he was in beer to cut his thirst. Each poison had its purpose, and he knew which he needed most now.

"You passing through?" The bartender stroked his long beard, then tossed it over his shoulder as he began washing glasses in a bucket. "Never seen you here before."

"Passing through," Slocum allowed. He sipped the beer. Although warm, it wasn't bitter and went a ways toward quenching his thirst.

"Not many jobs in these parts."

"Farming?"

"Alfalfa, hay, fodder for the horses on the ranches east of here. Nobody's getting rich, but nobody's hurting too bad either."

Slocum and the barkeep idly passed another half hour. Slocum finished a third beer and decided it was time to see if Angelina had settled in.

"Where's the Gomez house? A friend of mine's rooming there."

"All the way through town, left side of the road. About the best kept of the houses there. Has a broke-down wagon in the front but Elena—that's the señora—grows herbs under it. Uses it for shade from the summer sun. Hard to miss that."

Slocum agreed. He ran his finger around the rim of the mug once more and captured the last of the foam, then went to the door and stared out. It was still as bright and cloudless, but the tension he had felt before was so thick it felt as if a blanket had been dropped over the town.

Stepping out, he saw that the two men playing with the knife had brought around horses and left them in front of the bank. He found this passing strange because they stood just outside the door into the bank and whispered between themselves. Then they both pulled up their bandannas and whipped out their six-shooters.

Bumping into each other, they crowded through the door into the bank. Shots rang out.

Slocum drew his Colt Navy and started walking for the bank. The two robbers had to come out this way and would be easily captured. He lifted his pistol when the door exploded outward. He fired, jerking the shot high at the last possible instant.

"Robbery!" the man in the door shouted. "We're bein' robbed!"

The two outlaws shoved the man to the ground and grabbed for the reins of their horses.

"Stop!" Slocum fired again, but this time, in spite of aiming for the robbers, he missed.

The two mounted outlaws began firing wildly, sending lead in all directions. Slocum kept walking and firing, but the mounted robbers jerked around so much, every shot missed. Then they were galloping from town, heading west. He planted his feet, took aim, and squeezed off a final shot. He missed.

"Drop that iron, mister, or you're gonna get cut in half!"

Slocum looked over his shoulder and saw the barkeep with a long-barreled shotgun in his hands. The bores were trained on Slocum and looked big enough to stick his head into.

14

"I'll kill you where you stand if you don't drop that gun."

Slocum listened to the cold steel in the voice and knew there wasn't any chance to escape. Duck, dodge, it wouldn't matter to a man with steady nerves and a shotgun used to sweep up an entire saloon room full of drunks.

Slocum dropped his six-shooter.

He flinched when the shotgun roared, but the muzzle was aimed high. The discharge was intended to get people out into the street.

Slocum stood with his hands high in the air as he saw Marshal Hooker running down the street. The small man was sweating, and he waved around his six-gun.

"What's wrong?" the lawman yelled.

"Caught this one robbin' the bank, that's what's wrong," the barkeep said.

"He just rode into town with that widow woman," Hooker said, staring at Slocum. "You got a set of brass balls, using that woman the way you did to get me out of the way so's you could rob the bank."

By now employees had come from the bank. Two tellers

and a man dressed better than them who had to be the president came out, yelling and waving their arms like they could take wing and fly.

Slocum kept his mouth shut. There wasn't any reason for him to defend himself right now because he had to look guilty with his hands up in the air and an empty six-gun on the ground at his feet. He wasn't sure how he could talk his way out of it, but he might have a chance to escape when Hooker took him off to jail and there wasn't a scattergun aimed at his spine.

"I saw you had a hard look to you, but ridin' with that lovely woman threw me off. I ignored you and thought on her. I oughta string you up just for that," Marshal Hooker said.

"String him up all you want, Marshal, but get my money back!" The banker came over and continued to wave his arms around to no good effect.

"Where's the money?"

"His partners rode off with it. They left him when I came out," the barkeep said.

"What you got to say for yourself, Slocum? You tell us where those owlhoots are ridin' and might be I can cut you some slack—and I don't mean a noose, though you probably deserve it." The marshal came over and bumped his chest against Slocum's, looking up into his cold green eyes.

"I didn't do anything but try to stop the robbery," Slocum said.

"That's a likely story," the lawman scoffed. "Come on and—"

"Hold up there, Marshal. What he's sayin' is true. Me and him was talkin' over at the side of the saloon when them two varmints burst out of the bank. Why, Mr. Slocum here, he tole me he'd been robbed like that once and he wasn't gonna put up with nobody else bein' robbed."

Slocum glanced over his shoulder. He wasn't sure if he was surprised to see Herk. The man got around for being a gimp.

"That so, Slocum?" Hooker looked skeptical.

"What I said before is the truth. I tried to stop the robbery."

"No good deed goes unpunished, does it, Marshal?" Herk said, dragging his bad leg around so he stood off to one side. If shooting started, he would be out of the line of fire, from either the marshal's six-shooter or the bartender's shotgun.

"You swear to that?"

"Marshal, I protest!" The banker huffed and puffed and waved his arms some more. "That . . . that man might be part of the gang." He pointed at Herk.

"Naw, he ain't part of no gang," said the barkeep. "He comes and goes all the time and never had a bit of trouble with him."

"You come and go in Hedison?" Slocum asked. All he got from Herk was a smile that came close to being a smirk.

"Don't remember seeing him in town before," Hooker said.

"A week or two back he came through, said he was on his way to Abilene."

"Why'd you come back?" the marshal asked.

"Abilene's full of cowboys, and they don't always treat a man with my disability good, Marshal. Folks in Hedison don't laugh at me or shoot at my feet and make me dance."

Slocum heard a note of boredom in Herk's explanation, as if he spoke those same words repeatedly.

"Can I put my hands down, Marshal?"

Hooker frowned, then holstered his six-shooter and motioned for the barkeep to lower the shotgun.

"Reckon you got a good enough alibi. There's no way I can believe the like of him's taking part in a bank robbery," he said, dismissing Herk out of hand. "Might be the town owes you an apology."

"He didn't stop the robbery. Where's my money?"

"They rode due west," Slocum said. "The time it's taking for you to figure out I tried to stop the robbery, they might be in Mexico."

"Naw, that's too far," Herk said. "That direction, they'd

like as not go fer some waterin' hole. Lot of empty countryside that way. You know of a place like that, Marshal?
Where they could water their horses?"

"Ten miles down the road," Hooker said.

"Get a posse out there, you fool! Don't let them hide my
money!"

"Not exactly your money, Turnbull," the marshal said to
the banker. "More like the money of a lot of hardworking
men in town."

"How much did they get?" Herk crowded closer, rubbing
his hands as if he got to count the money himself.

"I don't know. I'll have to do an audit."

"How much, Turnbull?" The marshal's tone indicated he
wasn't taking any guff.

The banker looked at his two tellers, as if warning them
to keep quiet. Slocum saw the dollar signs spinning in the
banker's eyes, then fade. He sagged.

"Might have made off with a hundred dollars."

"Fifty in my till," one teller said.

"Not even thirty in mine," said the other.

"So it's eighty dollars those weasels stole. Hardly seems
worth the risk."

"Especially with a fine, upstandin' citizen like Mr. Slocum tryin' to stop 'em," Herk cut in.

"Get your horses," Hooker called to no one on particular.
"We're puttin' together a posse to go after a pair of bank
robbers."

"A ten-dollar reward," Turnbull said.

"Each?" asked Herk. Before Turnbull could say a word,
Herk cried, "Ten dollars on each of their heads!"

"I'll fetch my horse," the barkeep said. The tellers whispered to each other, then one indicated that he would go. By
this time a dozen of Hedison's citizens had gathered to see
what the ruckus was all about. Two more of them volunteered, the reward being more than they were likely to make
doing an honest day's labor in town.

"You, too, Slocum," Hooker said.

Slocum stared at him.

"I need you along. To identify the owlhoots."

"How many men are you likely to find on the road high-tailing it for Mexico?" he asked.

"I can identify them," the teller said. "Well, not their faces, but I remember what they were wearing."

"And the money'll be in a Hedison State Bank bag," Turnbull said. "They made them put the money in one of my moneybags."

Hooker started to say something. Slocum got the idea that there was no love lost between the marshal and the banker, but Hooker spun and went to get his horse.

Slocum and Herk were left alone in the middle of the street.

"You better get a' goin', Mr. Slocum," Herk said. "You don't want to fall behind. Ridin'. in this heat's hard enough without pushin' that fine gelding of yers."

"Why'd you lie?"

"You was innocent, weren't you? I couldn't let no tin star town marshal lock you up for no reason."

"I did try to stop the robbery," Slocum said.

Herk snickered.

"Course you did. What's the names of them friends of yers?" Herk hobbled off, holding his sides from laughter. Slocum bent, picked up his Colt, and reloaded it, wondering if a single shot to the back of the man's greasy-haired, balding head would be noticed.

He knew it would, but the urge stuck with him even as he slid his six-shooter back into his holster. The marshal rode up and silently pointed for Slocum to mount up. Without any choice, he did as he was bade.

"You sure they rode west?"

"Along the road, galloping until I lost sight of them," Slocum said. He might be mistaken since he hadn't been paying much attention to the robbers after the barkeep had gotten the drop on him.

"There's a hill a mile along the road where we can spot riders for another two-three miles. They can't have gotten too far," the marshal said with more confidence than Slocum felt.

"What if you can't find them?"

Hooker looked hard at Slocum. The answer was in his eyes. No matter what Herk had said, Slocum was the prime suspect for the robbery. He was sorry his aim hadn't been better. Leaving two dead men with bandannas over their noses and a sack of money clutched in their cold hands would have gone a long way to proving his innocence.

Now he had to catch the robbers and force them to admit they had acted on their own, that they had never seen him before.

Slocum hadn't paid much attention to them as they played mumblety-peg across the street from the bank while waiting for the right moment to commit the robbery. Thinking back, he wondered why they hadn't walked into the bank the first time he had seen them. Why give the residents of the town time to identify them before the robbery? It didn't make any sense, unless they were waiting for a signal.

Slocum glanced over at the teller, who rode easily. He might have been a cowboy at one time, come to town to find a life not as fraught with danger and hardship. Being a teller in Hedison probably paid as little as a range hand, but without the grub being furnished. That could be a powerful incentive to find a couple drifters willing to make quick money. Split three ways, eighty dollars wasn't much but more than they had at sunrise—and with little risk if the teller was the inside man giving the signal for the safest moment to start the robbery. Each would ride away with more than he'd earn in a month of punching cows and all for a few minutes of riskless robbing.

Or it might have been the other teller. Slocum got the feeling Turnbull wasn't much respected. He certainly wasn't beloved.

"How long has Turnbull had that one working for him?" Slocum asked as the marshal rode closer.

"How's that? Slick?"

"Slick? He used to be a card player?"

"Best there was, at least in Hedison. We got so few in town, they stopped wanting to play poker with him, so Turnbull hired him at the bank. I think he has Slick palm money and do all the card tricks with greenbacks that he used to do with cards. Never could prove nuthin'."

"He rides like a cowboy."

"He was that, too. Came from Indian Territory, I seem to recall. He's been in town for eighteen months or thereabouts, but he's not part of the robbery, if that's what you're intimatin', Slocum. He has a woman he treats right and who does well by him. Rumor has it Turnbull's fixin' on makin' him a partner in the bank."

"Why'd he do a thing like that?"

Hooker sucked on his teeth, then said, "Most folks don't notice it, but Turnbull's getting sicker by the day. He never said, but I suspect he's got cancer inside him, eatin' him alive."

"So Slick would inherit the bank?"

"Turnbull never married and doesn't have any people in these parts. Leastways none he ever mentioned."

They topped the rise the marshal had mentioned. Slocum reached around, brought out his field glasses, and carefully studied the road, then passed them to the marshal.

"Either they split up or there's another party moving away from the road."

"We do get travelers in these parts, Slocum," the marshal said. "We aren't that isolated since we're on the road to Abilene." He studied the dust clouds, then handed the glasses back. "My money's on the pair headin' south. That's where the watering hole is. Don't look like the ones on the road even know there's water within a hundred miles."

"If the robbers were just passing through, might be they wouldn't know about the watering hole."

Hooker shook his head.

"Not the way I see it. They probably didn't get as much money as they thought. A big enough take and they'd expect to have a posse after them. Leave fresh horses at a watering hole, they could outrun us."

"That's making them out to be a lot smarter than they looked," Slocum said. "It was as if the idea hit them, and they did it. No planning." Even as the words slipped from his mouth, he knew that wasn't right. They had waited. They were following a plan, but was it theirs? A pair of inept robbers could be manipulated.

"Men, that way!" The marshal snapped his reins and got his small posse trotting down the hill in pursuit of the men heading away from the road. Slocum kept up. It didn't matter if those were the robbers. He needed water, and so did his horse. If the stand of trees he spotted in the distance ringed a pond, he would be happy.

"They haven't spotted us, Marshal," the teller said.

Slocum studied the man closer. His long fingers were strong and nimble. He could see those hands holding a rope or dealing seconds from a deck of cards.

"No need to draw attention to ourselves by kicking up a dust cloud," the barkeep said. "We can sneak up on them and catch them when they camp."

Hooker worked on this, then said, "Good idea. No need to run them to ground. We can catch them since I'll bet they camp at the pond."

"How much?" Slick asked.

"How much what? Oh, that's not a real bet. Just a figure of speech," the marshal said.

Slocum saw that the gambler never left the man. Slick looked disappointed. Slocum wondered if he could get odds, then forgot about it when the marshal began forcing him away from the others in the posse to speak to him privately.

"You have the look of a man who can sneak up on them. You want to scout for us, Slocum?"

This surprised him. Hooker had gone from thinking he was a robber to giving him the chance to gather information that could make the arrest safer.

"I can do that. You trust me enough, Marshal?"

"Don't have much choice. Do any of them boys look capable of scouting like that?"

Slocum laughed. The lawman had a point.

"I'll circle wide. Give me an hour, then go straight in. I'll meet you with anything I've found."

Hooker nodded curtly, then rode back to the others. Slocum considered just keeping riding rather than spying on the robbers, but curiosity was enough of a goad to make him do as the marshal asked. He wasn't even certain the men at the watering hole were the pair that had robbed the bank. Finding out was part of an adventure.

He rode a ways before changing directions and approached the pond from the south so the men camped near the water were caught between him and the marshal. Slocum dropped to the ground, tethered his gelding, and then quietly advanced on the pond. The trees formed a green wall that hid him so that he came within a few feet of the men, now lounging back, boots off and feet in the water to cool off.

Slocum recognized them right away. The marshal's instincts had been right.

He slipped his six-gun from his holster but hesitated when one asked the other, "Think they got a posse after us?"

"Naw, we didn't get much. But that son of a bitch who shot at us. Was that the marshal?"

"Don't think so. We spotted the law earlier. Short drink of water, not like the sidewinder who opened up on us."

"Good thing he wasn't a better shot."

They laughed at this, making Slocum mad. He stepped out, his pistol leveled.

"Grab some sky," he ordered.

Startled, the robbers splashed about and looked around.

"It's them!"

Slocum swung around just as a rain of bullets sailed through the air and fell into the water, cutting a piece out of his hat brim. Then the outlaws had their six-guns out and blazing.

The death all around reminded Slocum of the many battles he had fought during the war, nobody aiming but intent on flinging, willy-nilly, as much lead out as possible.

15

Slocum added his own bullets to the sizzling hail as he dived
and landed hard on his belly. The impact caused his aim to
be off, but he still winged one outlaw. The man grunted and
grabbed for his thigh. He lifted his pistol to return Slocum's
fire and then began to shake like a leaf in a high wind. He
turned pale and toppled over.

"Got him!" came the shout from across the watering hole.
Slocum stayed on his belly. To stand meant he would present a target for the trigger-happy posse. Wiggling forward,
he got to the outlaw he had shot and saw why the man had
died so strangely. The bullet had ripped through the upper
leg and torn open the femoral artery. The blood hadn't
spurted out but had been soaked up by the man's jeans and
then drained down into his boot. Red fluid dribbled out over
the top of the boot, showing how much blood the man had
lost in a short time.

Slocum grabbed for the bank robber's six-gun. His Colt
was empty. Rather than take time to reload, he would use
the spare gun. His fingers slipped on the handle. Blood had
spattered everywhere. Slocum rubbed his hand in the dirt,

then picked up the bloody gun, rolled onto his side, and got off three more shots at the other outlaw, who was disappearing in the trees.

"You're lettin' him escape, Slocum," bellowed Marshal Hooker. The short man came running, his legs pumping like pistons on a locomotive. He held his six-shooter out straight-armed as he hunted for a decent target.

"Got one," Slocum said, tossing aside the outlaw's empty pistol. "We can run down the other."

"You let the sidewinder escape!"

"I had both of them dead to rights when somebody opened fire and spooked them. They thought they were going to die, so why not shoot it out?"

"That's a lame excuse," Hooker said, muttering to himself. Slocum knew the lawman was hunting for any reason to blame someone who was not a resident of Hedison for the escape. He had to live with them; he didn't have to put up with Slocum.

The teller, the barkeep, and the others crowded close, staring at the outlaw Slocum had shot down. They were silent. Likely they had seen dead men before, but in a quiet town like Hedison, there might not have been a violent death. That was for cattle towns like Abilene and Hell's Half Acre in Fort Worth, not a farming community where most men didn't even carry a sidearm.

"Where's the money from the robbery?" Hooker rummaged through the dead outlaw's gear, spilling out the contents of the saddlebags. He kicked at everything he had scattered about. "Not here. The money's not here."

"Reckon the escaping robber's got it, then," said Slick. He had recovered from the shock of the gunfight and looked around. "Can't imagine they would stash it around here, not with folks comin' and goin' all the time."

Slocum considered what the teller had said. It seemed incredible to him that the robbers had acted on their own. Two men that stupid would have been caught years ago, unless they had started on their life of crime in Hedison. That was certainly possible. They might consider robbing the bank a dress rehearsal for some bigger theft. From a safe, quick holdup in Hedison, they might decide to go to a stagecoach robbery or even try the bank in Abilene, where they stood to get away with a pile of money, not a paltry eighty dollars.

"You want to let them take care of things here so we can get after the other robber?"

Hooker stared at Slocum as if he had never considered such a thing.

"Might find him faster, just the pair of us," the marshal said, looking thoughtful. He gave the orders to the others to bury the dead man and wait for them. From the looks of relief, this agreed with them, though the barkeep had a question.

"We still get the reward?" He looked at the others. "We risked our lives. We deserve the reward."

"That'll be up to Turnbull—and if we can ride down the other outlaw," Hooker said.

"I think Mr. Turnbull will see fit to give the reward," Slick said. "I'll put in a good word for you boys."

Slocum snorted and turned away, working to reload his six-gun. Hooker quickly caught up.

"You thinking on claiming the entire reward for yourself?"

"I didn't even want to come along," Slocum said. "I'm here, I'll finish the job."

"So you'd be all right letting them split the reward?"

Slocum looked at the marshal and wondered what the fuss was over twenty dollars. The two robbers hadn't even made off with a big pile of money.

"It doesn't happen to us, not in Hedison," Hooker said, answering the unspoken question. "The good people talk about this kind of crime being so bad everywhere else, but not here."

"You up for election?"

"Real soon," Hooker said. "I like the job, I like the people. I worked as a deputy down in Houston for damned near a year and got shot at 'bout every day. That doesn't happen here. We don't even get many drunk cowboys because we're surrounded by farms, not ranches."

Slocum stepped up into the saddle and started on the outlaw's trail, letting Hooker catch up with him. The fleeing robber hadn't had time or the skill to hide his direction of escape. Slocum followed it at a trot.

"We got to grab him quick," said Hooker, galloping up. "If it gets dark, we'll lose him."

"He's running like a scalded dog," Slocum said. "He will run his horse into the ground in another couple miles. We'll have him then."

"I didn't see the other owlhoot's horse. He mighta took it, so he can switch off."

"There wasn't time. It surprised me he had the sense to take the money with him."

The marshal chattered on, making Slocum wonder if he was nervous about actually finding the bank robber. Within a mile his prediction came true. Hooker spotted the dead horse before Slocum, but that was all right. Slocum's quick eyes had discovered a different trail—boot prints going up a sandy hill and vanishing over the crest.

"There's his horse," Hooker said, but Slocum was already riding up the hill, wary of reaching the top. He didn't want to present a silhouette for a perfect ambush.

The boot prints went down the far side, but Slocum spotted the outlaw struggling along, hobbling a mite as if he had hurt his leg.

He let his horse pick its way down to the far side, then trotted after the outlaw.

"Your partner's dead," Slocum called out. "You don't want to end up the same way. All you did was stick up a bank. That's not worth dying for."

"You—you'd let me go if I gave back the money?" The outlaw held up the bank's money bag. "I don't want it."

"Drop your gun," Slocum said, not bothering to go for his own six-shooter. "The marshal's right behind me. He's a trifle nervy after the gunfight back at the watering hole."

"He'd kill me?"

"Don't give him a reason." Slocum felt no jubilation when the man dropped the money and threw his six-gun down on top of the money bag. The robber was a rabbit, not a wolf.

"You got him, Slocum? You got him?"

"Down here, Marshal. He's given up." Slocum pointed toward the sky. The robber's hands shot upward.

"Didn't hear any shooting," Hooker said, drawing rein beside Slocum. "He showed some sense and gave up?"

"Pretty much."

"Here's the money. It's all there. Ain't spent none of it." The outlaw nudged the bag with his boot.

"Haven't had a chance, you numskull. We got after you too quick."

"You let me go? You have the money and my partner's dead. Putting me in jail don't gain you nothing."

Slocum saw the argument had some sway over Hooker. A trial would remind the citizens of Hedison that their Eden had a snake in it. But Hooker also had to get reelected.

"Start walking," the marshal said. "We're goin' back to town."

"But—"

"Do it," Slocum said coldly. To Hooker, he said, "You see that the money's there. I'll keep him moving 'til you can catch up." He saw the marshal doing rapid calculation and knew what was foremost on his mind. "You can march him into camp at the watering hole."

This got a quick nod of approval. Slocum read the marshal's hesitation correctly. Hooker wanted to show his fellow citizens he was on top of crushing crime in their town. Letting Slocum take the credit for the capture wouldn't do, but that had just been taken care of.

The outlaw retraced his path, Slocum keeping a respectable distance. When they were on the far side of the hill, Slocum called out, "Put your hands down. They'll fall off your arms before we get back to town otherwise."

"Thanks. You're not such a bad fellow."

"You got that wrong. I'll shoot you where you stand if I have to. I might do it because I just want to. Why'd you do a damn fool stupid thing like rob the bank? I saw you and your partner waiting. What made you decide to go ahead with the stickup?"

"Me and Mel wasn't gonna get rich, but there was so much money waitin' fer us there, we couldn't pass it up."

"In Hedison?"

The robber looked confused.

"That's what we was told. A shitload of money was stuffed into the vault. It was empty as a whore's promise. We took what we could and then ran. Whatever we got woulda been all right, but it weren't no thousand dollars like he said."

"Who told you that?"

"The teller."

Slocum blinked.

"The teller told you all that money was yours for the taking?"

"Not in so many words. He was boastin' on it, and we're just flesh and blood men. Temptation got too big."

"What'd the teller look like?"

"He was in the bank."

Slocum described Slick.

"Naw, that's the other fellow there. This one was at the saloon and drunker 'n a lord. Shootin' his mouth off about how much money ran through his hands ever' day."

"So it was only the one teller who convinced you to rob the bank?"

"Can't say he convinced us. Didn't take much thinkin' on our part to come up with the idea on our own. We woulda never tried it if it hadn't seemed like the pot of gold at the end of the rainbow."

Slocum kept the man walking, Marshal Hooker saying nothing after he caught up. They returned to the watering hole. Slocum watched closely as Slick saw the robber hadn't been gunned down. There was a look of triumph on the teller's face that didn't go with getting drunk and setting the robbery into motion by telling a pair of drifters how much was stashed inside.

"Put him on his partner's horse," Hooker ordered. "We're headin' straight back to town. I ain't sleeping on the cold, hard ground because of him."

The others in the posse chattered like magpies, congratulating themselves on a successful foray. The marshal was happy enough and handed over the stolen money to Slick. Again Slocum watched closely. Slick seemed genuinely happy to recover the money and showed no concern over what the robber might say.

Somewhere around midnight they rode into Hedison. The marshal took his prisoner straight to jail, and Slick said he wanted to hand the stolen money to Turnbull right away.

"Drinks are on me, men," the barkeep said. He galloped to the saloon and hit the ground running. Inside his saloon were a half-dozen men nursing beers. Behind the bar a pallid woman drifted like a ghost. She brightened when she saw the barkeep, then the smile faded and she returned to her drab existence when he showed more interest in boasting about his role in capturing the desperado than in her.

Slocum leaned against the bar and accepted a watered-down whiskey as his reward.

"We done good, didn't we, Slocum?"

Slocum hoisted his glass and made a toast.

"To justice." He downed it in a gulp.

This set off a loud cheer, or as loud as the few gathered

in the bar could make. Slocum saw the other teller at the far end of the bar with a half-drunk beer. He went to the man.

"You ought to be happy. We recovered the money and caught the robbers," he said.

The teller looked uneasy.

"Reckon so. Terrible thing, robbin' a bank here. In Hedison, I mean. We're a peaceable community and things like this don't happen."

"How come you're not swilling the whiskey?"

"How's that? This is all I can afford. The whiskey was for the posse."

"But you got roaring drunk the other night. Can't imagine you did it on that weak horse piss."

"You're right about it being weak," he said with a smile. "But the other night was different, special." He smiled crookedly. "I was helpin' out with some tomfoolery."

"How's that?" Slocum motioned the barkeep over and ordered two whiskeys. Seeing the teller eyeing the second shot glass filled with amber liquid, Slocum pushed it toward him. "Join in the celebration."

"Much obliged."

"What was this joke you were playing?"

"Couple guys I never seen were here. A guy wanted to josh them some. Said he knew them and wanted to make them jealous. They came from some jerkwater town, and he wanted to make 'em envious of Hedison."

"You ever see the guys before?"

"Never did. Haven't since. Reckon they won't show their faces here after I bragged on how much money we had in the bank. We don't, but I was kinda drunk and it seemed funny then."

"Who was it playing the joke on the two?"

The teller scowled as he thought hard, then said, "Can't rightly remember. My brain was kinda foggy by then."

Slocum started to question the man further but the barkeep started in telling about the gunfight at the watering hole. His role expanded to be the central one. Slocum wasn't going to call him a liar. Let him enjoy his moment in the sun.

Slocum turned and leaned on the bar, both elbows supporting him. Not ten feet away in the rear of the saloon sat a man he knew all too well—and maybe not at all. Herk concentrated on every word the bartender said. His eyes glowed and he was breathing a mite faster than usual.

The teller pushed away from the bar and said, "Thanks for the whiskey. It went down real good. Wish I coulda gone along like Slick, but Mr. Turnbull, he needed me to keep the home fires burnin', so to speak." He took a step, then stopped and said to Slocum, "The man what played the joke on them two the other night? That's him in the back of the room." He walked out on unsteady legs.

Slocum and Herk stared at each other. Slocum doubted it was too hard for Herk to read his mind. The crippled man got up and scuttled out the rear door into the night.

16

"You're quite the hero," Angelina said, moving closer to Slocum. Her hip pressed hotly into his as they sat on the bench staring out into the main street. Sounds from the kitchen behind them put Slocum on edge. Worry over what the townspeople would say about Angelina and an unmarried man sitting so close together in a restaurant was foremost in his thoughts.

Almost foremost. He saw Herk hobbling along the street, occasionally talking earnestly to people. Some brushed him off but others stopped and listened.

"What's he saying?" Slocum wondered aloud.

"John," Angelina rebuked. "I was paying you a compliment, and you weren't listening to a thing I said."

He looked at her. She was prettier than ever. The night's sleep in a decent bed had done wonders for her.

"Is the señora going to let you stay?"

"Why, I didn't ask. She is very nice. Her husband is, too. I spoke with him about getting a lawyer—*abrogado*, as he called it—and he steered me to one right away."

Slocum wondered if it was the marshal's nephew or the

other lawyer. Somehow, selling the ranch had faded in importance, at least to him. He craned his neck but lost sight of Herk. For a man with a game leg, he certainly moved around fast.

This thought made Slocum frown. Something didn't seem right, and he couldn't put his finger on it.

"John!"

"Sorry, I was thinking about the bank robbery."

"I heard that you tried to stop it, and when you couldn't, you volunteered to be deputized and ride after the crooks."

"I killed one of them," he said bluntly. Angelina recoiled at this.

"I had heard the shooting was done by the bartender."

"He claimed it, but I wasn't more than ten feet from the robber." Slocum snorted in wonder. "I wasn't even trying to hit him, not like that." He pressed his forefinger down on Angelina's thigh and said softly, "That's about where I shot him by accident."

"Really," she said, her bosoms rising and falling a little faster. "Would you shoot me there? Or take aim here?" Her hand gripped his and moved it up and over toward her crotch.

They both jumped when the waiter came with their breakfast.

"Here you go. If you want salt or pepper, just ask. I got 'em both in back. Too many customers steal the shakers." The waiter laughed. "That's usually what passes for crime in Hedison."

"Looks good," Angelina said, but her eyes weren't on the steak and eggs in front of her. She stared at the bulge in Slocum's jeans.

"Want anything else, just ask."

"Good advice," Slocum said.

"Yes, John, if you want anything else, you just ask."

"I intend to." He dived into the food, eating with the hunger that had built from missing too many meals recently.

Halfway through the steak, he paused and pointed with the tip of his knife.

"You know him? The short fellow."

"The one with the bad leg? Why, yes, I think I remember him. He and Michael argued once in Abilene."

"Over what?"

"I can't say. Michael was furious, and he never told me. There . . . there was hardly time for such things before he was killed."

"Don't you think it's curious he turns up in Hedison?"

"I suppose. Why do you care, John?"

Slocum didn't have a good answer for her. Something about Herk bothered him. It was like an itch he couldn't quite scratch. It wouldn't go away, and even if he did reach it, there wasn't likely to be any relief.

"Somebody got a teller drunk."

"I beg your pardon? What are you going on about?"

"Never mind," he said. "You about finished with your breakfast?"

"I am still hungry, if that's what you mean."

The sly smile curling her lips matched his own. He fumbled in his pocket and found a greenback. It fluttered to the table. He helped Angelina scoot across the slick bench seat, aware of how her ankles showed as she moved. It had been a while and he wanted to see more of her than the well-turned ankle or a bit of calf. Showing her where he had shot the outlaw would be part of it, if he could press his finger into her milky white thigh before moving up into a more dangerous—and pleasurable—area.

"We can hardly return to the boardinghouse," she said. "The bed is so delightful, but too many people are there all the time. There are three children, you know."

"I didn't know—that," he said. His arm snaked around her waist and pulled her tightly to his body. "I know a lot of other things."

"Don't tell me, show me!"

"You've sure gotten pushy," he said.

"Not pushy, horny," she said, moving closer and nibbling on his earlobe. Slocum tried to look around to be sure no one saw them, but with his earlobe caught between her sharp teeth, he wasn't able to do much looking. "And you can certainly get some pussy," she whispered. She immediately latched on to his ear again.

They walked on until she had to give up her tasty treat.

"There," he said.

"Where? The windmill?"

"It's pumping water. There ought to be a small house holding the gears and pumping mechanism where we can get some privacy."

The blades on the windmill creaked as they spun in the sluggish West Texas wind. From deep below the ground came sucking sounds as the pump brought water to the surface and spewed it out into a large tank. Slocum worried that this was the town water supply and citizens would come by to fill barrels or buckets and find them.

Then that thought disappeared as Angelina reached down and boldly grabbed his crotch. He moaned softly as he grew under her rhythmic movement, grasping and relaxing.

"In," she said. He didn't know what she was referring to, but he could do both.

They swung around. He kicked open the door to the shack, revealing the gears and pump he had expected. What was unexpected was a cot along the far wall of the shed. As if it were a magnet and they were iron, they went directly to it. She pushed him down and dropped between his legs, her fingers fumbling to open the buttons of his fly.

Slocum sighed in relief as his erection popped free of the cloth prison, then gasped when her soft lips closed around the very tip and began applying suction. Bit by bit, inch by inch, she moved closer to him, taking more of his steely length into her mouth. He felt the underside of his organ rub across her wet tongue and then she made a convulsive gasp and took him full length. He sagged back, supporting himself on his elbows as she continued to use her mouth in exciting ways all over him.

With a lewd *pop!* she pulled away and looked up at him, blue eyes glowing.

"More," was all she said.

He was willing.

She stood and lifted her skirts. He caught his breath as she slowly revealed more and more of her legs. The trim calves, the milky thighs, the tangled black nest hidden between her legs. He lay back on the cot. It creaked under their combined weight as she straddled his waist.

Her fingers closed around him and tugged hard, lifting him off the bed so she could position herself directly over him. Slocum watched as the plum tip of his manhood parted her pinkly scalloped nether lips and then slowly disappeared into her hot moist core as she lowered herself. When she had fully relaxed, he was hidden full length within her.

It was even better than having her tongue and lips moving and kissing. When she began tensing and relaxing her inner muscles, she gave him a massage that excited him almost to the breaking point.

"Move," he said. "Move up!" He grabbed her tits and began massaging them, then pushing her upward until she got the idea. Through half-closed eyes, she looked down at him. Angelina put her hands on his shoulders for leverage and lifted herself even as he continued to fondle her.

He felt himself slipping from her tightness, then she paused and slowly lowered her hips again. Once more he was fully buried within a wanton, willing woman.

He moved from her breasts to the spot at the top of the vee where her nether lips joined. He found the tiny spire there and began pressing into it with his thumb. It was as if he had set her on fire. Her movement began to jerk and twist as she lost all control. She cried out, rose, slammed back down. The inner oils leaked from her. He used these to slicken the tiny spire, stroking it with every twitch she made until she finally threw back her head and cried out at the top of her lungs.

He felt the tightness within his loins growing, but he didn't want her to stop. With deft movements he urged her to keep pounding up and down, engulfing his spire, turning around it and then lifting again. Her arousal mounted once more, and the second time she got off, he did, too.

The hot rush exploded upward into her yearning cavity, and the world disappeared into a starburst of utter pleasure. Then she slowed her frantic movement and leaned forward. Her legs stretched out along his and she lay atop him, her head resting on his shoulder. He felt her slow, warm breath against his neck.

"So nice, John, just what I needed."

"Can't argue with that. It was about perfect."

He stroked her tangled hair and turned a bit so she could lie alongside him rather than on top. As he adjusted his position, he saw a blur of movement at the half-closed door to the pumping shed. He started to push her aside and track down whoever had been spying on them, but she clung too fiercely to him.

"Don't go, not yet," she said in a whisper. "I need you more now than . . . than before we started making love."

He had no choice but to hold her, listen to the mechanical sounds all around—and let the Peeping Tom go his way.

"We better go," Angelina said after a spell. She heaved a deep sigh, snuggled a little closer, then pushed herself up using Slocum's chest as a base. Her blue eyes danced. "I wish we could . . ."

"Time to go," he agreed. He watched as she stood and arranged her skirts, sharing her wish that they could stay here for another hour or so. But the clanking from the pump warned that it was getting close to breaking down. When it did, somebody would come to fix it, even if that repair was no more than slamming a sledgehammer against it a couple times.

Angelina peeked out the door.

"See anyone?" he asked. She jumped.

"Why, I wanted to make sure that . . . no one. Why? Did you expect to see somebody? Watching us?" Her tone combined both fear and excitement at the idea of being watched while she screwed.

"What are you going to do?"

"Find the lawyer," she said. "The sooner I get the ranch sold, the sooner I can do . . . something else."

"Hedison is a nice town," Slocum said, fishing a bit to see what her thoughts might be.

"I don't know what I could do. I'm not much of a cook. My sewing skills are poor." She grinned. "The one thing I do might not be illegal, but it's not what a proper lady does."

"You do a couple things well," Slocum said. He got her moving, almost pushing her out into the hot sun. Even in direct sunlight, it was cooler than inside the shed. Heat boiled out from the machinery as it ground up and down, pulling water from deep under the prairie. Slocum craned his neck and looked up at the windmill. One blade wobbled. It would fall off in a week or if a high wind blew from the south.

"Let's get together later, John." She hesitated, then stood on tiptoe and gave him a quick peck on the cheek. She actually blushed, looked away, and then hurried off. Angelina looked back over her shoulder an instant before rounding a building and heading down the town's main street to find the lawyer.

Slocum wandered around, looking for any sign of who might have been spying on them in the shed. He found faint boot prints in the dust but couldn't be sure when they had been made. From the condition of his and Angelina's prints, they all were made about the same time. Backtracking, Slocum measured the stride and guessed the spy was about five-foot-five. One strange thing was how the right heel had been cut down—he tried to remember where he had seen a print like that and couldn't. Any other information was lost by the time he got to the street. Too much traffic had effectively erased the trail.

He preferred tracking in the wilderness. There other people weren't as inclined to wipe out the tracks. More than this, there wasn't the noise even a town as small as Hedison generated. The clank of chains and creak of wagons going by in the street were dimmed by the whinny of dozens of horses and the sounds of everyday commerce.

It was early, but he headed across the street and went into the saloon. The barkeep was pressed close to the pale-complected waif who had taken over bartending duties while he had been on the trail of the bank robbers. He looked up, saw Slocum, and flashed him a grin, then turned back for a final word with the woman. She bowed her head and left through the rear door.

"Top o' the morning, Slocum. You're in early for a beer."

"It's getting hot enough for a couple," Slocum said. He waited as the barkeep slid the frothy brew toward him. A quick sample and he put the mug down on the bar. "That your woman?"

"Clara?" The barkeep's cheerful disposition faded as if a cloud had crossed the sun. "You might say that. She's not a whore, if that's what you're asking."

"Farthest thing from my mind. You trusted her to run the saloon while you were gone. That's all I meant."

"She came to town a month back, down on her luck, without two nickels to rub together. I gave her a job."

Slocum guessed it was more complicated than that. From the woman's complexion, she didn't sample the liquor but dipped into laudanum a bit too much. It wasn't his business.

Two farmers came in and the barkeep hurried off to put beers in front of them. They took their drinks to a table and sat, genially arguing over something inconsequential. From what Slocum could tell, they were in town to pick up supplies from the general store.

As he worked on his beer, the two farmers left, joshing one another. Slocum finished his beer and followed them into the street a few minutes later, to see the two squaring off.

"You can't say that about me!"

"What the hell are you talkin' about?"

"Talking behind my back, you son of a bitch. I never touched that little girl!"

"My niece? You and her?" The farmer balled his fists but he was too late. The other farmer launched a haymaker that collided with the man's belly, sending him stumbling back.

The two launched into an all-out fight. Slocum took a couple steps toward them but remembered what had happened when he tried to stop the bank robbery. This was something best left to the marshal.

But the tenor of the fight changed fast. One farmer pulled out a wicked thick-bladed knife and cut the air just a fraction of an inch from the other's belly.

"What's got into you?" demanded the unarmed one.

"You can't go around lyin' about me."

"I never said a word!"

The knife drove forward but was batted away at the last instant. Slocum saw a spray of blood, though. Fighting a man with a knife meant blood would be spilled. A man afraid of taking some injury was sure to die. The only way to survive was to ignore the pain and concentrate on getting the knife away from the attacker.

The two circled, the knife wielder making tentative stabs and slashes. Then everything changed. A strong hand against Slocum's shoulder blades sent him stumbling forward between the two. He cried out in pain as the knife cut deep in his side and he lost his balance, falling to his knees between the two enemies.

Slocum called out for them to stop, but all he saw was the silver blade flashing in the sun and driving straight for his face.

17

The wound in his side burned like a prairie wildfire, forcing Slocum to jerk as he put pressure on it. This saved his life. The blade missed his face and got stuck in his hat brim. As he tumbled downward, the knife flew out of the farmer's grip. Slocum hit the ground, clutching his side in agony.

"What the hell's goin' on?" The demand was followed quickly by a gunshot.

Through a red haze of pain, Slocum saw Marshal Hooker bustling up.

Even the presence of the law didn't stop the two men from fighting. One kicked Slocum in the side where he was wounded as the man grabbed for the throat of the other farmer. They went down in a tangle because Slocum reached out and used his arms to embrace their legs. If they had worn spurs, he would have been cut up even more than he was. Instead, he brought them crashing down like felled trees.

He rolled away, still clutching his side to stanch the blood flowing freely now. He looked up and saw Herk not ten feet away. The man had an expression that would have been more reasonable if he'd just had the finest woman in all of Texas in his bed. His eyes locked with Slocum's. Herk sneered, then turned and vanished into the crowd forming along the street.

"Glory be, Slocum, you got the worst of it," Hooker said. He grabbed Slocum's shirt and pulled him upright. "You just keep on pressin' into that wound. We'll get the doc here right away."

"Ain't got a doctor in Hedison," someone said. "He's the vet."

"Suits me," Slocum said. He bundled up his vest and shirt, using them as bandages. For all the blood, the cut wasn't that serious. Painful, to be sure, and bloody enough to make the marshal think he was dying.

But he would live. And he'd find out what he had blundered into the middle of.

"How'd you come to get involved?" a man asked. He dropped a large satchel, opened it, and took out diabolical-looking medical instruments.

"You the vet?"

"None better," the man said. He fumbled about inside and pulled out scissors. In seconds he had a large patch of Slocum's vest and shirt cut away. With a gentle touch that no human doctor ever shared, he peeled back the blood-soaked fabric and began tending the cut itself. "You're going to need a few stitches."

"Do it," Slocum said.

"Get him out of the sun." The vet looked down at Slocum. "That's not to make you more comfortable. No way you can be comfortable with that cut. It's because the sun reflects off my suturing needle. You want some whiskey? I can send for it, but I'll have to charge you extra."

"Stitch me up," Slocum said. He winced as the carbolic acid burned away at the wound, but it was numb by the time the vet began sewing.

"I'll close it up with more sutures than I need so you won't have a scar, though that doesn't look like much of a concern." The veterinarian ran his hand over Slocum's side, fingers tracing out several existing scars.

"You done?"

"There," the vet said, snipping off the thread. "You'll be good as new in a week. Sooner, if you don't ride or do anything to tear open the cut."

"How much do I owe you?"

The vet looked at him thoughtfully, then said, "I'll put it on your bill. You've got the look of a man who might qualify for a discount because of quantity." He closed his valise, talked to Marshal Hooker, then sauntered away as if nothing had happened.

Slocum sat in the shade, his side aching now rather than hurting. He tossed aside his shirt and vest. No amount of cleaning or sewing would repair them.

"John, I heard the commotion. I should have known you'd be in the middle of it. Were you trying to be the hero again?" Angelina stopped and stared at his bare chest. Blood still smeared his side and the wound was beginning to pucker around the stitches. "Are you all right?"

"Been better," he said.

He got to his feet and went to the marshal. Hooker held the two farmers apart, stiff-arming them both. They snarled and hissed and spat like a pair of fighting tomcats.

"You two cool off, or I'll throw you both in the clink," Hooker said. This hardly settled them.

Slocum took care of the matter. He swung a roundhouse that doubled over one farmer. He recovered his balance and sent a flurry of jabs into the other's midsection, dropping him to his knees and holding his gut.

"You shouldn't have done that, Slocum. Now I got to run you in for disturbin' the peace." The marshal wilted under Slocum's glare. "Might be this was self-defense, you gettin' stabbed and all."

Slocum grabbed one of the men by the collar and pulled him up until their faces were only inches apart.

"What started the fight?"

"He's been lyin' 'bout me!"

"How do you know?" Slocum asked. He shook the man like a terrier would a rat trapped in its jaws.

"I was told, that's how. How do you think I'd know?"

"Who? Who told you he's been spreading lies about you?"

"That gimpy little wart. The one what came to town a month or two back and showed up again a couple days ago."

Slocum heaved, sending the man to the ground. The other was fighting to regain his breath.

"You know Herk?" he asked this farmer.

"That little fella? I seen him around. Not so much after I tossed him out on his ass when he came sniffin' 'round my wife a month back."

Slocum let him go and turned to the marshal. He fought to keep his anger in check as he said, "The cause of all this is the man calling himself Herk. I don't know what that's short for. Maybe nothing. He gets men drunk and then watches them fight. He spreads rumors and outright lies. This is what he wants."

"Why? Just because Luke chased him off a month back?" Marshal Hooker looked confused at the sudden turn of events.

"That might be all, but I suspect he enjoys watching men fight and die. It makes him feel big to be in control—and they don't know it. He's the finger on the trigger but never the bullet."

"Can't arrest a man for talkin'," Hooker said.

"Might be he was the one who convinced the two they ought to rob the bank. Talk to your prisoner real good and find out. He said somebody set it up for them, and they couldn't refuse because they thought there was a thousand dollars in the bank."

"How come they'd ever believe someone like Herk?"

"Because he liquored up the teller and convinced him it was a joke on those two. A teller spills his guts that there's a fortune in a small-town bank, no guards, not much of a vault, and even a man used to robbing banks would listen. Two drifters who'd never robbed anything other than a candy jar in a store when they were kids would believe that story."

Hooker went on to protest, but Slocum paid him no attention. He tried to fit everything together that had happened to him. Angelina said her husband and Herk had argued. Herk had a penchant for lovely ladies, or so it seemed, and a bigger one for causing trouble for their menfolk. Slocum had to wonder about Macauley getting gunned down.

That had all the earmarks of what he thought Herk did. Somebody passed along to the cowboy that his wife was cheating. Might have been, Herk picked a hotel room number at random. But did he get Finch to gun Macauley down, or did he do it himself just for the thrill of the confusion it caused? Slocum had seen the glint in Herk's eyes when he saw men fighting. He was like a drunk with a new bottle of rye whiskey as he listened to how the bank robber had been gunned down.

Confusion, yes, but more. Fights, deadly ones, and even murder all seemed to thrill Herk.

And Slocum had no way of proving any of it. Who'd believe a man with a game leg could get around that much?

"You need to get out of the sun," Angelina said, taking his arm and pulling insistently.

Slocum looked around before he let her lead him away. He had the eerie sensation of being watched—and he knew it was Herk. It had always been Herk, but how had he managed to move so fast, so agilely?

"Did you ever talk to him? Herk?"

"Not really. When he came by that one time, he only spoke to Michael. Argued with him."

"Did your husband know Macauley? Or Finch?"

"I suppose he did. I know he and the marshal were friends. He always called him Willie. Well, maybe not friends, but they knew each other well enough to be on first names."

"Trying to figure out where all the strands go of the web Herk is spinning is too hard," Slocum said. His side ached more by the minute, and he was getting a little woozy. He had felt this way before so it wasn't anything that worried him unduly. When Bloody Bill Anderson had shot him in the belly and left him for dead on William Quantrill's orders, he had felt much worse. It had taken months to recover. This was hardly a scratch compared to that wound.

"You're making a mountain out of a molehill," she said. "So what if he is a Paul Pry and sticks his nose everywhere? That doesn't make him a killer."

"He's worse. He's like a vulture. Never kills anything himself but is always there when something dies. He feasts off the misery of others. The difference is the buzzard doesn't help matters along by lying to the rabbit about the location of a watering hole or telling a blacksnake that an owl is its best friend."

"This is shock from your wound making you talk this way. Come along. I will see if there isn't a spare bed or cot where you can lie down. Señora Gomez might even let you stay in my bed."

"But not for long," Slocum said.

"Not overnight. She is a very religious lady, and she has children."

They went to the Gomez boardinghouse but all the señora would allow, in spite of Slocum's wound, was to bed down in the barn. That was plenty good enough for him.

Señora Gomez fussed over him even as she chased Angelina out to go find her lawyer.

"You rest. I have water for you here," the woman said. "Would you like food? I can prepare another place at dinner."

"That's all right. Just give me a place to stretch out," Slocum said. He heard the charity in Señora Gomez's offer but also the strain it would place on her family feeding another, even for one meal.

"If there is anything, ask," Señora Gomez said.

"One thing," Slocum said as she turned to go. "A man with a bad leg. Did he try to rent a room from you?"

She looked at him curiously before answering.

"How is it you know this? *Sí*, such a man did ask a week ago."

"But you didn't rent him a room. You couldn't have or there wouldn't have been one for Angelina—Mrs. Holman."

"He made me uneasy, but I found him a place. It is not as nice as my house, but it suited him."

"Where's that?"

"An old house on the far side of town, east toward Abilene. The Edson family lived there for many years but all died of food poisoning." The disdain in her voice told Slocum she blamed the adults in the family for the sickness. "It is not a place filled with disease. Not like plague, but no one wanted to stay there."

"So he might be staying without paying anyone?"

"That is so," Señora Gomez said. "There is no one to pay rent to." She pointed to the pallet on the straw she had laid out.

Slocum dutifully stretched out, wincing only a little as his tense muscles began to relax. By the time the woman had left the barn, he was almost asleep.

Almost.

Herk kept haunting him, the left leg dragging behind— or was it the right? Slocum painfully sat up and concentrated. Which leg did Herk favor? He couldn't remember, and that bothered him because he had seen the man hobbling about often enough.

"East of town," he said softly. "East in an old house."

Gripping a broken board in the stall, he levered himself to his feet. A moment of giddiness passed and he left the barn, taking care not to be seen. Señora Gomez was not one

to anger by rejecting her hospitality, but Slocum had to find
out what he could about Herk. The man had mysteriously
appeared at the damnedest times.

And the shadow he almost saw from the corner of his
eye too many times. It had moved faster than a crippled man
ever could, but which leg had Herk injured?

Slocum retrieved his horse, mounted, and rode slowly
through town. He kept a wary eye out for Herk, but the man
was nowhere to be seen. Before he reached the outskirts of
Hedison, Slocum checked his six-shooter to be sure it was
loaded. There was no telling what trouble he'd ride into if
Herk was at his home.

He rode for another ten minutes before seeing a weathered, knocked-over sign proclaiming EDSON RESIDENCE.
The small road shooting straight back to the ramshackle
house afforded no cover. The prairie was flat, and he would
have to wait until sundown if he wanted to approach the
house without being seen.

He rode directly to the house.

A quick circuit showed where a horse had been tethered,
but the animal was gone. Feeling luckier than he had
recently, Slocum dismounted gingerly, favoring his side. It
had stopped aching and now filled his entire body with a
throbbing like a tooth going bad. As long as he didn't outright hurt, he could draw his six-shooter in a flash.

He went up the three steps onto the porch. Two of the
risers were missing and one step had broken through, rotted
in spite of the dry air. He pressed his ear against the door
and listened for any sound inside. Only the faint creaking
of the house responding to his weight on the front porch and
the soughing of wind through cracks in the walls could be
heard. The doorknob felt cool to his touch. Slowly turning,
he waited for some reaction from inside.

He flung the door open, hand resting on his six-gun. Only
the wind disturbed the quiet interior. The Edsons had died
fast, or so Slocum guessed. It was as if they had simply left

one day and never come back. The rocking chair in the far side of the room had knitting on the seat, everything thick with dust. Two plates had been set out on the table, but there wasn't any silverware. Slocum poked around and found another plate that had been used recently, wiped clean, and then placed beside the woodstove.

A cast iron pot sat atop the stove. Some wood had been stacked beside the potbellied Franklin along with a bucket of water. With the wind and heat, that water would have evaporated in a day. That meant Herk had been here recently, maybe sleeping until daybreak and then going into town in time to lie about one farmer to another and see the fireworks.

Slocum touched the long, shallow knife cut on his side. He might have died from that. And then another memory returned, one he had forgotten because of the fight and his injury. A hand had rested between his shoulder blades an instant before he stumbled into the middle of the fight. He had been pushed.

He continued to prowl around the room. A pile of newspaper pages carried recent dates. Slocum touched one page and was surprised when he found the ink smeared. Pushing the sheets around, he couldn't figure out what newspapers the pages had been taken from. He remembered that the *Hedison Gazette* was a weekly paper. The pages might have been taken from it, but the articles dealt with goings-on in Abilene.

Slocum held one page out and saw where a single article had been clipped out. From context he couldn't tell what it was. He tossed aside the paper and continued to hunt—but for what? He wasn't sure but would know when he found it.

His search finally brought him around to the bed, where an old Army-issue blanket had been tossed on top of the mattress. He peeled back the blanket and saw a large book. He picked it up and recognized a family album. But instead of pictures, the pages had newspaper clippings pasted on them. Holding the album up to the light, Slocum tried to read the first article, but the ink had faded and the paper had long since turned yellow.

Flipping through, he discovered more recent clippings. As he read them, he grew angrier by the minute. On the last page, he found the article from the *Hedison Gazette* about how Marshal Hooker's posse had gunned down one bank robber and brought back his partner.

Each of the clippings was about a death, a murder, or some other crime. Slocum started to toss the album down when he saw faint markings in the margins. He thrust the page out into bright sunlight and saw the penciled notations. If Herk had been there when he finished deciphering the crabbed writing, he would have shot him down without a second thought.

Beside each clipping Herk had written comments about how excited or disappointed he was in the death. One man had been sent to prison for three years. Herk had hoped to see him lynched.

The notes led Slocum to believe that Herk had instigated the crimes described in each article. Slocum had all the proof he needed to be sure Herk deserved to die for the crimes he had provoked. But it wasn't legal proof. He was convinced, but a judge would dismiss any charges because of a lack of solid evidence.

Slocum stomped from the house, not sure how he'd stop Herk but positive that he would.

18

Slocum stepped out of the shack and looked around, squinting in the blazing sun. He had a prickly feeling that he was being watched. The only one likely to be out here and intent on him was Herk, but Slocum couldn't find a place where the man might be hiding. He walked around a bit, hunting for a hidey-hole or somewhere that Herk could squeeze his small frame into, but he found nothing.

Slocum rode back to town, feeling a bit woozy. He wanted to ask some questions and find out what the people in Hedison knew of Herk, but he was almost falling out of the saddle. He headed back to the Gomez house and dismounted, expecting to be caught and scolded like a wayward schoolboy. Wherever everyone was, they weren't watching for him. He went into the barn and sank to the pallet. The outline of his body from when he had lain here before was still impressed into the blanket. He fitted himself into that outline again and expected to rest for a moment.

When he came awake, it was dark. He panicked, thinking he had gone blind. Then he settled down and realized the sun had set. The cool breeze blowing through the open door assured him that he had slept most of the day. Carefully stretching, he found that he was stiff and a bit sore but otherwise in good shape. He stood, his legs stronger now than they had been earlier when he had gone hunting for Herk's lair.

The house was dark and nobody answered when he rapped on the door. Slocum rode back into town. The saloons were booming now. He tried to remember if it was Saturday night again. The days had slipped away from him, and the entire day spent sleeping had done nothing to let him figure out what day of the week it actually was.

He grinned crookedly. Not having to be at work at a specified time or day robbed him of his sense of the day of the week. It felt good not having to be tied down even that much. Working a ranch, there was never a break in the week except Sunday church services. Otherwise, one day followed another and looked no different.

Finding a spot to hitch his horse, he went into the saloon. It was packed to the walls, the barkeep working to keep the beer mugs full and the pallid woman, Clara, doing what she could to pour whiskey and make small talk with the customers. He settled down with his back to a wall. Eventually Clara made it to him.

"Whiskey?"

"Give me a beer," Slocum said. He was running short of money. Better to pay a nickel for a beer than a dime for a shot of the whiskey.

She turned and floated away like a ghost on the wind. Slocum leaned back and discovered he was still tired. His eyelids drooped, only to pop open when a commotion at the door awakened him.

"You little snot," bellowed a man the size of a mountain. As he moved into the saloon, Slocum decided he was closer to being the size of a mountain range. He held a farmer by the front of his shirt and lifted him up on his toes. "You don't say nuthin' to Big Bill Bozeman. You unnerstand?"

"Yes, M-Mr. Bozeman!"

The huge man flung his captive across the room, knocking over two others.

"I said you don't speak to me. And you did." He growled like a grizzly and lumbered toward the hapless farmer.

"What kin I git you?" Clara asked. She interposed her slip of a body between Bozeman and the prone farmer. "You look like the kind who can hold his liquor, so I bet you want whiskey. The rougher the better."

"Yeah, I don't want none of that sissy smooth stuff. I want it to taste like sandpaper goin' down."

"Come on over, try the house special. It's got nitric acid in it. Don't reckon anybody else here's man enough for a drink with such a mule's kick."

Slocum approved of the way Clara maneuvered the huge man and got him to forget about beating up on the farmer, whose only crime was trying to leave as Bozeman entered. She was worth whatever she was getting paid if she could keep the peace within the saloon walls like she had just done. Knocking back the last of his beer, Slocum made his way through the crowd and stepped out into cool night.

He looked around, expecting to see Herk. But the small man had made himself scarce. Slocum doubted he had moved on, though Herk seemed to spend a lot of time going between Hedison and Abilene, plying his vicious rumors so he could watch the deadly results.

"John! John!"

He turned to see a flustered Angelina hurrying toward him, waving a paper in her hand.

"Have you seen this?" She thrust out the newspaper until he took it from her.

"Haven't paid attention to the local news. What's got you het up?"

"This!"

He held up the paper so he could read in the light coming over his shoulder from the saloon. The print was smeary and small, but his anger mounted as he worked his way down the front page of the *Hedison Gazette*.

When he'd finished, he stepped closer to the light and read the article again.

"That . . . that man can't say things like that about me. About us!"

"Doesn't bother me what others call me. A pimp is about the least of what some have said about me over the years, but calling you a 'traveling whore' and a 'two-bit soiled dove' is libel."

"Libel. Yes, that's the word! I wasn't able to get a lawyer to handle the sale of the ranch because both of them in town said it would tarnish their reputation representing me!"

"Why'd the editor print this?" Slocum folded the paper and tucked it under his arm. The pressure of his arm against his wounded side gave him a different kind of pain now, but his outrage that any newsman would print such lies about Angelina pained him more.

"Let's find out," Slocum said.

"He can't print tripe like that. He can't." She was close to tears.

Hedison wasn't so large that Slocum couldn't find the small newspaper office in a few minutes. A single coal oil lamp burned inside. He heard mechanical clanking, telling him a new edition of the *Gazette* was being printed.

He tried the door, but it was locked. He rapped loudly but got no response.

"Wait here. I'll see if there's a back door."

As he rounded the small building, his hand flashed to his six-gun. An indistinct form moved away at great speed, a shadow blending into a shadow. The man had left the rear door ajar so that a tiny sliver of light dribbled out onto the ground. Slocum started after the fleeing man, then stopped and pushed open the door to the newspaper's storage room. The smell of printer's ink and newsprint made his nostrils flare. He stepped inside, moving carefully through the haphazard stacks of supplies.

Another door led into the print room. A portly man with an ink-stained apron worked to place every sheet of paper, then screw down the printing plate before peeling back the freshly printed newspaper.

"You the editor?"

The man spun about, then scowled.

"You made me smear the page. Takes forever to dry. I need some of that fast-drying ink they use over in Abilene, but it costs an arm and a leg. Who the hell are you?"

Slocum walked through the print room and opened the front door to let Angelina in. He turned to face the editor.

"I'm the man you lied about, and this is the woman you're trying to ruin. Care to explain?" Slocum held out the newspaper Angelina had given him.

"I don't know you. Either of you."

"That didn't keep you from writing terrible things about me. About us!" Angelina stepped forward. "Those were all lies, every last column inch of it."

"Column inch?" The editor looked hard at her. Slocum didn't see the lust in the editor's eyes that most men showed when they looked at Angelina. Instead, there was an appraisal that went to what she said. "You know about the newspaper business?"

"I know you print terrible typographical errors . . . in addition to the lies!"

"You found mistakes? I copyedit my own work!"

"Forget that," Slocum said. "Your paper will get Mrs. Holman run out of town on a rail—and she hasn't done anything, much less the things you accuse her of."

"I have proof. I never print a word that isn't backed up with solid facts!"

"What proof do you have that I'm a pimp? That Mrs. Holman is 'a Cyprian who goes from town to town pleasuring the lower class of males?' I think I got that line right." Slocum didn't bother looking at the page. He balled up the newspaper and tossed it into the corner, where an already tall stack of discarded sheets threatened to topple over.

"You're Slocum?" The editor thrust out his chest and puffed himself up. "I'm not afraid of you!"

"You ought to be!" Angelina blurted out. "He's the one who caught the bank robbers. Shot one and tracked down the other one for the marshal."

"That's not what Marshal Hooker said. And Boyd shot the bank robber."

"Boyd?"

"The bartender. If you'd been there, you would have known."

"Never heard his name before, but if you press Boyd about it, his story might change. And the marshal's up for reelection, so he'd claim he caught the other robber. Fact is, he was the only lawman in the posse since he didn't deputize any of us."

"He didn't? That'd mean what Boyd did might have been manslaughter, not being a lawful deputy trying to arrest a bank robber."

"I am not a whore!" Angelina suddenly shrieked at the top of her lungs, silencing the two men. Tears running down her cheeks, she balled her fists at her sides and stamped her foot like a bull getting ready to charge.

"Got proof you are, though you don't have the look."

"Not like Clara, over at the saloon?" Slocum said.

"She does have the look of dipping into drugs a bit more than most," the editor said.

"Why not write that . . . that tripe about her?" Angelina still sputtered in her anger.

"Because I got proof you're a whore." His words were defiant, but Slocum heard some doubt creeping in. Angelina wasn't acting like a soiled dove. If anything, such a woman would revel in the publicity for the attention it would bring her.

"What is it?" Slocum kept his tone level.

"You're Slocum? And you're Mrs. Holman, of course. Yes, of course."

"And you're Josiah Hightower," Angelina said.

She had paid more attention to the details of the article than Slocum had. Putting a name to your enemy helped keep the fight in perspective. He silently applauded her for such keen observation.

"I am. It's irregular for you to come to my office. I have a paper to get out."

"Your next edition will carry a full retraction and an apology," Angelina said. "I will accept no less."

"Here, look at these," Hightower said, pulling out a folder crammed with newspaper clippings. "I am merely reporting what has already been stated in other papers. Why, here's a damning piece from the Abilene paper." He held out a long strip cut from a newspaper.

Angelina snatched it from him and read down.

"Why, this is all lies, too."

"Is it from another newspaper?" Slocum asked. "Or is it a fake article?"

"It's from another paper. How can it be fake?"

"You have a telegraph here in town. Find out. Wire the editor over in Abilene."

Hightower looked at Slocum strangely and finally said, "Why do you think it's a fake?"

"None of that ever happened, that's why," Angelina broke in. She subsided when Slocum shot her a silencing look.

"She's right. More than that, the paper is brand spanking new. Is the ink even dry?"

"What's that—oh, it's supposed to be six months old." Hightower ran his fingers over the paper, then held it up and crinkled it. "Not newsprint either. A better paper than any frugal publisher would use. How do you know these things?"

"I found a book filled with clippings. I thought they might be souvenirs, but then it came to me they were all fairly new. Dates were wrong for the paper and ink. I've seen what a newspaper looks like after being in the sun for a day. These were kept nice and purty."

"You mean the articles are all lies?"

"Wire the editors of the papers those clippings supposedly came from. I know what you'll find. And it's all lies about Mrs. Holman and me."

"You wouldn't ask me to send those 'grams if a one of these came back true, would you? No, you wouldn't run a bluff like that 'cuz you know I'll do that very thing!"

"I—we—want a full front page retraction," Angelina said.

"Don't much care," Slocum cut in, "what you say about me but the lady's reputation is at stake."

"And I want to copyedit the page to be sure you don't put in those terrible misspellings again."

"You ever work at a paper?" Hightower asked.

"Why, no, but I'm asking to clear my name."

"I need somebody who can go over the stories and make sure my English is intact and the words are spelled right. You need a job—provided I get back telegrams saying none of what I'd been shown is right?"

Angelina looked at Slocum, then said, eyes wide and sparkling, "I would love to work for you, Mr. Hightower."

"Call me Josiah, or if you want to be more formal, call me Editor Hightower. I'd like that. Never had an assistant before."

"Senior editor," Angelina said. "Perhaps I can even write a story or two." Seeing his reaction, she said, "It's not unheard of having a woman reporter. Why, in Saint Louis they—"

Slocum left the two of them discussing the news trade.

He slipped into the street and looked around. Asking Hightower to describe the man who had given him the bogus newspaper clippings wasn't necessary.

It had to be Herk. And Slocum needed to do something about him. Soon.

19

The house was empty. Slocum poked around using the barrel of his Colt Navy to push aside debris, but nothing he had seen before that he identified as belonging to Herk was to be found.

Herk had moved on.

Slocum sat on the edge of the bed, trying to figure out where the gimpy little son of a bitch would run. The only place that made any sense was back to Abilene. Herk bounced around like a child's ball, from one town to another, spewing his lies and making a passel of trouble for whoever suited him. Slocum wondered if he had been chosen for a reason or if it had all begun with Macauley's death. Herk had poured the poisonous lies into the cowboy's ear and picked a hotel room at random. Slocum happened to be in the room, innocent of everything boiling around him.

The best Slocum could figure, Herk had actually shot Macauley down—whether to watch him die or to add more fuel to the flames hardly mattered. Macauley was dead, and Slocum was swept up in a flood of lies and death that got worse by the day.

He knew that Hightower would get back the truth when his telegrams were answered, but how had Herk gotten the clippings so specifically damning Slocum and Angelina if he hadn't written and printed them himself?

"Abilene," he said under his breath. There were a couple newspapers there. Herk could have set the type and printed the bogus sheet himself after breaking into either of them—or even both after the editorial staff had left for the night. He might have done up an entire page, then cut the articles apart and made them look as if they'd come from different newspapers. The man was nothing if not cunning.

Slocum had to keep telling himself that Herk was also very dangerous. He didn't have to pull the trigger; all he needed to do was make someone else believe the lies and they would do the killing for him.

For his sick pleasure.

Slocum stood and started to leave when something shiny caught his eye. A knife lay half-hidden under a chair. He picked it up and had a curious sense of having held it once before. Turning it over and over in his hand, he was slow to remember where he had seen it before.

"Son of a bitch," he muttered. He slid the knife into the top of his boot when he heard scraping sounds outside.

Slocum knew better than to rush out, even with his six-shooter drawn. The sound was likely to be a lure for a trap. He stepped back, looked up, and saw a hole in the ceiling. With a jump, he caught the edge of the hole, winced at the pain this caused in his side, then pulled himself up and into an attic. The roof was only inches above him as he crawled along, but he soon came to a ventilation hole he could peer from.

Crouched below him, a pistol in each hand, Big Bill Bozeman waited impatiently for his quarry to pop out the front door. If Slocum had gone out to investigate the noise, Bozeman would have opened up with both six-shooters.

A million thoughts raced through his head. Bozeman

might be hunting for Herk. Somewhere, somehow, Herk had made a misstep and had a reward levied on him. But a bruiser the size and ferocity of the bounty hunter wouldn't consider gunning down a man with a game leg who hardly came to his shoulder. If he brought back quarry like that, he would become a laughingstock. From what Slocum had seen in the saloon, Bozeman wouldn't tolerate any disrespect, much less mockery.

He wasn't after Herk. He was after John Slocum.

A coldness settled on him when he remembered Herk's warning that a bounty hunter was on his trail. Slocum had brushed it off, but this had to be another of Herk's deadly schemes. He might have sent for the bounty hunter immediately after alerting Slocum.

Looking down, he saw no quick and easy way to escape. It would have been an easy shot from Slocum's vantage. He could put a bullet smack on the top of Bozeman's head, and the bounty hunter would be dead before he hit the ground. Even if he had a skull like a grizzly bear, he would be very, very dead at this range.

Slocum considered a parley if Bozeman was on someone else's trail, but he didn't think the bounty hunter was the talking kind after the fight back at the saloon.

Before he could consider another course of action, Bozeman shot to his feet, ran to the front door, and kicked it in with a sound like a gunshot. The bounty hunter roared and went stomping through the house. Slocum had heard quieter wild horse stampedes. A few shots tore through the ceiling behind Slocum, but he didn't budge. Bozeman vented his wrath at not finding his quarry, nothing more.

In a minute, the bounty hunter stomped from the house and looked around. Slocum held his breath when Bozeman spotted Slocum's gelding out by the barn. The huge man laid a gentle hand on the horse's neck, then looked around with a gimlet stare. Slocum lay still, watching intently. He had to shoot it out if Bozeman took his horse, but that would be horse thieving and Slocum would be within his rights to keep his own property.

To his surprise, Bozeman laughed harshly, then strutted away. He thrust the two six-guns into his broad leather belt and vanished into a ravine. Slocum heard a horse galloping off shortly after.

He caught the edge of the opening, turned himself about, and dropped feet first to the ground. The impact sent a jolt of fresh pain into his side, but he ignored it. Bozeman had something in mind, and Slocum wanted to find what it was. He thought of the bounty hunter as a thread in a bigger tapestry. Tug a little on this thread, and he might trace back to the design Herk was weaving.

Herk had to have done something wrong that a marshal would find illegal.

Trailing the giant bounty hunter wasn't too difficult. His horse tired after a few miles, letting Slocum close the gap between them. He still hadn't figured out what he was going to do when he lost the trail.

One instant it was as plain as the nose on his face. The next it disappeared like smoke in a high wind. Slocum circled the area, trying to understand how he had lost the trail so quickly. After twenty minutes he had no idea. Bozeman must have known he was being followed and done something to throw his tracker off. What that was, Slocum was at a loss to say.

He sat and considered what the bounty hunter might do, then coldly considered everything he knew. Herk wasn't the bounty hunter's victim; he was. Slocum knew that Bozeman had recognized his horse outside the barn and must have decided to lure his prey to him rather than continue hunting and maybe catch a bullet in the gut.

Slocum was sorry he hadn't shot the man in the head when he'd had the chance, because the only bait that was sure to draw Slocum was back in Hedison.

Angelina Holman was in danger from the bounty hunter.

Slocum put his heels to his horse's flanks and galloped across the countryside, taking a shortcut to get back to town as fast as he could ride. The entire way he cursed himself for trying to play Herk's game—Bozeman's game. He had outsmarted himself, and if he was right, Angelina would pay for it.

Hooves flashing, he rode down the middle of the main street before skidding to a halt in front of the *Hedison Gazette*. He hit the ground running and threw open the door. Hightower had not bothered locking it, possibly because it was early enough in the morning that no one would disturb him unduly as the townspeople went about their business. He had claimed only gossip showed up in late afternoon, when it got too hot to work but not to talk.

"Hightower! Where is she?"

The portly editor looked up from his desk, a small smile on his face.

"She's excellent, Slocum, most excellent. She caught several—"

"Where is Angelina?"

"What's wrong?"

Slocum didn't have time to answer questions. He needed them answered. He turned to go, but Hightower called after him.

"She finished copyediting the next edition and said she was going home. I assume that mean to her boardinghouse."

Slocum vaulted into the saddle and pushed his tired horse the half mile across town to Señora Gomez's house. As he neared, he slowed and hunted frantically for any sign that Bozeman had used Angelina to trap him. He didn't see the bounty hunter's horse, but the barn door stood open. That wasn't like either of the Gomezes, though one of the children might have been careless.

Slocum didn't think so.

He dropped from the horse and let the reins dangle. It wouldn't go far, not when there was a rain barrel beside the house. The gelding went straight for it to drink. Slocum would have stayed to make sure it didn't drink until it bloated, but he had bigger fish to fry. He slid his six-shooter from his holster and warily advanced on the barn.

Pressing his back against the wall, he chanced a quick glance inside. In the brief instant he looked, his heart almost exploded. Angelina had been strung up, hands tied above her head and her toes barely touching the floor. The pain would increase every second he left her there. Worse yet, Bozeman had stripped her naked to the waist. Her blouse hung in tatters.

Rather than barge straight in and probably get himself filled full of lead, Slocum edged around the barn until he came to a dirty window. He used his elbow to clear off a spot in the lower right corner of the pane, then dropped to his knees and pressed his eye to the clean glass. As he had thought, Bozeman waited, pistols drawn, just to the side of where Angelina hung helplessly. Slocum would have died the instant he entered the barn.

He lifted his pistol to fire, then lowered it as a better idea came to him. Returning to the front of the barn, he avoided the door. Bozeman was sure to fire at the slightest movement. He scooped together a small pile of dried horse dung and stacked dry straw on top. It took him a few seconds to light the pile. It fitfully flickered, then the straw began to burn. In a minute the dung would catch fire. He hurried back to the rear of the barn, found a small door, and opened it slowly to avoid any creaking sound that might betray him.

By the time he slipped through into the barn, the fire he had set was filling the air with the stench of burning dung. Bozeman left his hiding place and went to the door, cursed, and ducked outside.

Slocum slid up behind Angelina and clamped his hand over her mouth to keep her from crying out.

"I've got proof Herk killed your husband. A knife exactly like the one used to kill Michael was in his gear," he said.

"Herk planted the knife he used in Barnett's belongings to frame him." He let loose of his hold over her mouth. "If you don't set Bozeman on Herk's trail, I'll have to shoot him down. He's been duped like the rest of us."

"Wh-What do you want me to say?"

"Tell him Hightower has proof Herk is a killer and has a reward on his head for killing Macauley."

"He . . . he killed him, too?"

"Has to be," Slocum said in a low voice, doubting Finch had done the deed. Herk had stirred the pot even more by killing Macauley.

"That horrible man did . . . this to me!"

"He's been lied to. Stop Herk. If you get Bozeman on his trail, I won't have to kill him. Otherwise, I don't see any way of stopping a bounty hunter with dollar signs dancing in his eyes."

He ducked back as Bozeman returned.

"So damn hot, fires start all by themselves," he muttered.

"You're after the wrong man," Angelina said.

"Now, if you don't keep your mouth shut, I'll have to gag you. Don't want you scaring off Slocum."

"Herk!" The name exploded from her lips. She rattled off all Slocum had told her. At first Bozeman didn't believe her, but from where Slocum watched through two ill-fitting planks in a stall, the bounty hunter looked increasingly curious.

"So you don't mind me leavin' you all trussed up and gagged while I go ask this editor fellow what he's discovered about Herk?"

"Of course I do," Angelina flared. "But if it's the only way you'll believe that Herk is a killer and there's a reward—a big one—on his head, I'll do it."

"How big?"

"Marshal Wilson in Abilene sets the amount. I don't know."

Again she hit the right note. If she had given Bozeman

too much detailed information, he would have been suspicious.

"This Slocum fella, he don't have a reward on his head?"

"He's a cowboy, nothing more," she said.

Bozeman sat and thought a spell, then got up and stuffed a rag into Angelina's mouth, fastening it in place with a length of rope looped around her head.

"You better be tellin' the truth," he said. Bozeman took one long, last look at Angelina's naked breasts, then left.

Slocum waited until he heard a horse galloping off before coming from his hiding place. It seemed fitting to use Herk's knife to cut her bounds. She fell into his arms, and he lost his balance, tumbling backward into a stall.

Angelina plucked the gag from her mouth but didn't get off him.

"You're sure that Herk killed Michael? How did that misshapen little—"

"A lot about him has bothered me from the first. He knew my name when there wasn't any call for him to, and which leg does he drag behind him?"

"Why his—" Angelina frowned. "I've seen him limping along on both his left and right."

"So have I. I don't think he's crippled at all. That's his way of seeming harmless while he spies on people and tells his lies. He drags his right foot more, and that wears down the heel. That ties him to another crime—he was there at the stock pond when Ralston kidnapped you."

"Why does he do it?"

"For the sick pleasure it gives him. He's in control of other people's lives and there's nothing they can do. I saw how he looked when two men were fighting. Bloodshed excites him, especially if he is the cause. It's an even bigger thrill if nobody knows."

"I can think of bigger thrills," she said, her expression unreadable.

"What?"

"The bounty hunter will be on the trail. He won't come back to free me, will he?"

"I doubt it."

"Then I can reward you for saving me. And finding Michael's killer. And that cowboy's, Macauley."

Slocum started to say this hardly seemed the place, but she kissed him hard on the lips, silencing him. Her breasts pressed down warmly against his chest, then she began moving about, rubbing her nips across him until they were hard enough for him to feel through his shirt.

"Suckle them," she said, rising up. He saw the hard tips, engorged with excited blood, pulsing with every rapid beat of her heart. He strained until his lips brushed over the tender morsels. He kissed them, used his tongue to roll the pink beads about, and then sucked hard, getting first one and then the other into his mouth. He gave them his full oral attention even as Angelina worked to free him from his jeans.

When he popped free, she twisted about and took him in her mouth. He pushed away her skirt and exposed her privates. As she straddled his face, he reared up and thrust his tongue into her depths. A powerful shudder passed through her body and she sagged. For a moment.

Then she scooted down his body and got to her feet, still facing away from him. She hiked her skirts and spread her legs just enough to give him a view that excited him to the point he almost exploded.

He came up to his knees and pressed his face between the creamy half-moons of her ass and licked, then stood and gripped her around the waist. She leaned forward, hands against the top of the stall to brace herself.

His hips thrust forward, and he bounced off her lust-moist pinkly scalloped lips. She groaned with pleasure, reached back between her legs with one hand, and guided him to the spot where she wanted him most.

"There?" he asked.

"There!"

She let out a shriek as he began moving inward, slowing sinking into her from behind. Tight, tighter than he had ever imagined, hot enough to burn steel, she surrounded him. When he was fully within her, he simply relished the sensation. Then she began rotating her hips. In tiny circles at first and then in bigger movement that stirred him around within her like a spoon in a mixing bowl.

"Do it hard, John, hard and fast. Do it!"

He withdrew slowly, making sure she was stretched wide enough for him, then he obeyed his own body rather than her words. But the result was the same. He slammed hard into her, feeling her fleshy cheeks press into the circle of his groin. He began thrusting with as much passion and energy as he could, the friction mounting until he was sure he would melt.

She cried out in release as he plunged far into her, then he knew he wasn't far behind. He swelled within her closeness, then let flow the white tide burning its way out of his loins.

They slammed together, parted, and went back together in a perfect fit, then Angelina sank to her knees.

"No . . . no more," she said. "I'm still on fire inside. Never felt like that before—ever."

Slocum rocked back on his heels, then sat heavily. He was drained, exhausted, and agreed completely with her.

Only one thing would be better. And he would see to that soon enough.

She came to him again, this time their lovemaking slower after expending so much energy the first time. Only the return of Señor Gomez disturbed them—until they could find a more secluded spot to finish.

20

"Smelly fellow, yeah, he was here," said Josiah Hightower. "He asked funny questions, but I gave him the straight as an arrow information. It seemed to make him mad."

"You get the telegram back from Abilene?" Slocum asked.

"You know that already. I can tell by the look you're giving me. It was all you said. And a second 'gram to a friend of mine confirmed that Herk is there. Seems Marshal Wilson has his hands full with fights and even another murder."

"Herk do it?"

"I asked the Abilene city editor about that. One cowboy shot another in plain sight of a dozen witnesses. Nobody knows what set it off. The one that did the killing clammed up and isn't saying a word, other than the dead man deserved it."

"Herk found out something damning," Angelina said, "and used it to blackmail the man who did the shooting. If he speaks up, he'll reveal the very thing he wants to hide. That's a terrible crime!"

"Herk will tell everyone what the secret is, if he can get

a lynch mob together because of it. Or something even bloodier. He does like the bloody spectacle," Slocum said. Why he hadn't incited a mob to burn down a town was a puzzler for Slocum. Or maybe Herk had done that somewhere else before coming to Abilene. He might enjoy the more personal bloodshed. What went on in his head was a complete mystery to a man like Slocum, who only wanted to be left to himself and chose not to meddle in other people's affairs as long as they left him alone.

"You two surely do consort with evil folks." Hightower shook his head.

"Did Angelina tell you about this?" Slocum dropped Herk's knife on the table.

"Same brand as what killed her husband from what the lady says, but that doesn't prove a thing," Hightower said. "Might be a dozen men bought the same kind of knife from a traveling peddler. Or there could have been a deal at the general store. I've seen sales like that." Hightower picked it up and made a face. "Crappy knife. Cheap. No way a merchant would remember who bought this, even if it was bought recently in Abilene."

"True, but suspicious," Slocum said.

"You need more."

Slocum smiled. There might well be nothing more he needed to do since Bozeman had been put on Herk's ass.

"I'm riding to Abilene," he said. He saw Angelina start to speak, then press her lips together thoughtfully. "You don't have to go," he said. "Might be best, in fact, if you stayed here out of the gunfire."

"You'd shoot down Herk?" Hightower spoke as if it was an accusation rather than a question.

"Won't have to," Slocum said, but he would if it came to that. Herk was a poisonous snake biting people when they least expected it. Too many had died, either by his hand or through the rumors he spread. He had to be stopped, and Slocum wasn't sure getting him thrown in jail was enough.

Herk would find a way to lead the prisoners in a jailbreak and spread his venom even more by playing on their anger.

"But you would, if you have to?" pressed Hightower.

"I want to stay, John." Angelina spoke up, rescuing him from lying to the editor. "Mr. Hightower—"

"Josiah," he cut in.

Angelina nodded in acknowledgment and continued, "Josiah has asked me to work on the *Hedison Gazette*."

"She's got quite the eye," he said. From the way Hightower looked at her, he was interested in more than her eyes. Slocum didn't blame him.

"I can correct errors and do some fact checking. There's no reason for . . . Josiah to take the time to send telegrams and do work like that when he is better employed writing and printing the newspaper."

"Don't see why she can't do a story or two either," Hightower said. "From the samples I've seen of her writing, she's as good as any reporter in Texas."

"Sounds like it'll be the leading paper in West Texas before you know it," Slocum said. He wanted to kiss Angelina good-bye but wasn't going to, not with Hightower standing so close and giving him a cold, hard look.

Slocum tipped his hat and left. It was a couple days' ride to Abilene, and he spent it thinking about Angelina—and finding Herk.

He felt like a thief in the night sneaking into Abilene, but Slocum wasn't sure what reception he would get. Herk might have forgotten about him or might have made him a life's work by spinning more innuendo and outright lies. A cowboy like Finch would buy it if he still believed Slocum had killed his friend over a woman.

Slocum dropped into a chair outside a saloon so he could listen to some of the talk inside. The night was cold so nobody thought anything about his sitting with his arms wrapped around him and his hat pulled down low over his eyes. He might have been sleeping off a drunk for all anyone knew.

He tensed when he saw the marshal coming down the street, heading straight for the saloon, but Wilson didn't give Slocum a second look as he pushed through the swinging doors. The noise inside dropped to where Slocum could hear a pin drop.

"Where is he? Where's Bozeman?" Marshal Wilson didn't sound happy with the bounty hunter.

"Last I seen, Marshal, him and Finch was across the street. They had their heads together like they was plottin' something important. You want I should tell him you're lookin' for him?"

Wilson stormed out and went across the street to another saloon. Slocum followed, making certain he didn't do anything that would alert the marshal that he had picked up a shadow.

He stood just outside the doors and looked inside to where Wilson had found the men he sought.

"I don't want none of this foolishness like you're sayin', Finch," the lawman said.

"You won't believe the evidence. This here's a famous bounty hunter. He don't make mistakes—like you."

"I follow the law, and you ain't got nuthin' to pin on Herk. As far as I know, he's a law-abidin' citizen."

"Over in Hedison, they got proof he killed that Holman fella," Bozeman said. "They got the knife and everything."

"I have the knife, numbskull," Wilson raged. "Doc matched the broke-off tip with the blade found in Barnett's gear. Damned shame him gettin' lynched, but he done the crime. I'm as sure of that as I can be of anything these days."

"Bozeman here says Herk shot down Macauley. He was my best friend."

"Didn't take you no time a'tall to move in with his widow," Wilson said.

"She was grievin' and needed comfortin'. I'm supplyin'

that for her," Finch said defensively. "You said it couldn't have been that Slocum fellow what shot Mac. We been askin' 'round and Herk was—what's the term?"

"Incitin' to riot," Bozeman said. "We found the folks he talked to and got them to repeat what he said. He was lyin' to make Macauley all angry to kill somebody."

"And it wasn't Slocum what shot him. It was Herk."

"You ever seen Herk? The little shit's got a bad leg. He couldn't shoot Macauley like that and run away as fast as Slocum claimed. It'd take somebody with a damned fine pair of legs to get down those backstairs that fast."

"He done it," Finch insisted.

"You do the askin' 'round, Marshal? This here Herk, does he have any warrants out on him?"

Wilson started to speak, then shook his head.

"Found a man matchin' his general description, but that one had two good legs."

"Might be he just hurt hisself," Finch said.

"Might be you and this mountain of gristle and stupid are makin' up stories. You jist want ever'thin' to be all right so you can marry Macauley's woman without nobody thinkin' she's a whore fer gettin' hitched so quick after Mac died."

"Now you listen here, Marshal. You got no call to say that about Martha!"

The argument started. Slocum looked around for any sign of Herk. This was the kind of potential bloodshed that drew him like a buzzard to carrion out in the desert. When he didn't see him, he looked down the street expecting to see a fast-moving shadow. Slocum didn't see any such thing, but he did see the light on in the window of the newspaper office.

He went down the street and cautiously peered inside. Herk sat at a table sliding lead slugs onto a strip. Slocum wondered what lies were being concocted for yet another set of bogus newspaper clippings. He looked down the street and saw Marshal Wilson dragging Finch out of the saloon by his collar. Bozeman followed, protesting the arrest.

The trio would pass in front of the newspaper office in a few seconds. Slocum drew his six-shooter, went around back, and found that Herk had already jimmied open the door. That didn't stop Slocum from kicking it in to make as much noise as he could.

"Herk!" he shouted at the top of his lungs and pointed his six-gun directly at the startled man at the table.

Herk shot to his feet and threw a tray of the heavy lead slugs at Slocum. He ducked, ran to the front door, and dashed into the street. Slocum shouted again, this time for Marshal Wilson.

Looking through the open front door, Slocum saw that the marshal was torn between his prisoner and looking around.

"Bozeman, he's getting away. Run him down!"

The bounty hunter was huge, but he was quick and recognized the fleeing Herk. He caught the small man ten yards down the street and dragged him back, kicking and fighting.

"There ain't nuthin' wrong with his legs. By damn, Bozeman, you're right!" The marshal released Finch, who began screaming about how Herk had killed Macauley. Within seconds a crowd gathered.

Slocum slipped out the back door of the newspaper office amid cries for tar and feathers. Finch demanded a necktie party, and Bozeman wanted the reward. Whatever happened to Herk, it wasn't going to be good enough—but it would do.

Going to his horse, Slocum mounted and considered riding back to Hedison. Then he reconsidered. There wasn't any good reason to make the return trip since Hightower would hear about tonight's goings-on from the Abilene editor. Angelina Holman was a mighty fine-looking woman, but she had found a job at the *Hedison Gazette*, and unless he was mighty wrong, Josiah Hightower would ask her to be more than copy editor and sometime reporter soon enough. If he didn't, he was a fool.

Slocum didn't think he was.

He rode straight south out of Abilene, knowing he would find the road leading to San Antonio eventually, but right now letting the cold Texas night engulf him, the silence soothe him, and the bright stars above guide him—those were enough.

DON'T MISS A YEAR OF

Slocum Giant
by
Jake Logan

**Slocum Giant 2004:
Slocum in the Secret
Service**

**Slocum Giant 2005:
Slocum and the Larcenous
Lady**

**Slocum Giant 2006:
Slocum and the Hanging
Horse**

**Slocum Giant 2007:
Slocum and the Celestial
Bones**

**Slocum Giant 2008:
Slocum and the Town
Killers**

**Slocum Giant 2009:
Slocum's Great
Race**

**Slocum Giant 2010:
Slocum Along
Rotten Row**

penguin.com/actionwesterns

M457AS0510